Ho-Ho-NOOO!

TJ and the TIME STUMBLERS

BOOK 4
Ho-Ho-NOOO!

Bill Myers

Tyndale House Publishers, Inc.
Carol Stream, Illinois

Visit Tyndale's website for kids at www.tyndale.com/kids.

Visit Bill Myers's website at www.billmyers.com.

TYNDALE and Tyndale's quill logo are registered trademarks of Tyndale House Publishers, Inc.

Ho-Ho-NOOO!

Designed by Stephen Vosloo

Edited by Sarah Mason

Published in association with the literary agency of Alive Communications, Inc., 7680 Goddard Street, Suite 200, Colorado Springs, CO 80920, www.alivecommunications.com.

This novel is a work of fiction. Names, characters, places, and incidents either are the product of the author's imagination or are used fictitiously. Any resemblance to actual events, locales, organizations, or persons living or dead is entirely coincidental and beyond the intent of either the author or the publisher.

For manufacturing information regarding this product, please call 1-800-323-9400.

ISBN 978-1-4143-3456-1

Printed in the United States of America

17 16 15 14 13 12 11
7   6   5   4   3   2   1

To Michael Lau. Thanks for your help
and diligence these many years.

CHAPTER ONE

Beginnings . . .

TIME TRAVEL LOG:

Malibu, California, December 18

Begin Transmission:

Subject is not fond of video games. I, on the other hand (spit-spit), am not fond of geraniums.

End Transmission

"Fire proton torpedoes!" Captain Tuna shouted.

"Aye, aye, Captain!" the ever-loyal (and always dim-witted) Lieutenant Herby called back. But before Herby could reach over and push the button labeled

WARNING: Push only if you want to blow stuff up and make a real cool mess!

their spaceship was struck by a powerful explosion. The craft lurched violently to the left and was suddenly filled with the sounds of

"Row, row, row your boat—"

"Oh no!" Captain Tuna shouted.
"Oh what?" Lieutenant Herby shouted back.
"He hit us with the Stupid Song Bomb!"

"—gently down the stream."

Not only was the entire spacecraft filled with the silly stupidity, but so were the brains of the entire crew (i.e., Tuna and Herby—well, actually, only Tuna for sure, since medical science has yet to determine if Herby has a brain).

"Merrily, merrily, merrily, merrily—"

"Augh!" Captain Tuna cried, grabbing his head in agony.

"Groovy!" Lieutenant Herby said, tapping his foot in ecstasy.

"Raise the deflector shields!" Captain Tuna shouted.

But Herby was too busy singing along to hear the orders.

Another explosion hit, throwing the craft to the right.

*"Twinkle, twinkle, little star,
How I wonder what you-"*

Captain Tuna leaped from his chair and staggered toward the control panel. "Must . . . stop . . . the . . . music!"

But before he arrived, they were hit again.

*"Jack and Jill went up the hill
to fetch a pail of-"*

And again.

*"Here we go round the mulberry bush,
the mulberry bush,*

the-"

Just when Tuna was about to lose his mind (leaving the spacecraft with a grand total of zero minds), the singing was interrupted by an even worse sound.

"Greetings, zwork-oids!"

Tuna spun around and gasped. There, on the giant viewing screen, was the vilest of all villains, Bruce Bruiseabone. He stood on the bridge of his own spaceship, laughing his creepy

"moo-hoo-ha-ha-hee-hee-hee"

laugh.

Captain Tuna watched in horror as the villainous man put his villainous hands on his villainous hips and spoke (what else?) villainously.

"And so, my mini-micro-minds, we meet again."

"What do you want from us, you fiendish fiend?" Tuna shouted.

"I want you to hand over the keys to your spacecraft."

"Never!"

"What?" Bruce shouted back. "You dare challenge me, the most villainous of all villains?"

"That's right!" Tuna yelled defiantly.

"We're the heroes of this story," Herby explained, "and heroes always win!"

"Have it your way." Bruce turned to one of his crew members and shouted, "Fire torpedoes!"

Once again the ship lurched, and Tuna's brain (and whatever there was of Herby's) filled with

"The itSy-bitSy spider crawled up the water—"

"AUGH!" Tuna *augh*-ed.

"Shh," Herby *shh*-ed. "This is my favorite part."

"Down came the rain and waShed the Spider—"

"Not only will you hand over your keys," Bruce shouted again, "but you will give me those giant foam dice hanging from your rearview mirror."

"Oh no!" Tuna cried. "Not the foam dice!"

"Guys?" a female voice suddenly called from below. Another bomb struck:

"Are You sleeping, are You sleeping? Brother John? Brother-?"

"Guys!" The female creature stuck her head up through the spaceship's floor. She had dark hair, wore glasses, and was incredibly smoot (at least according to Herby—well, all right, according to Tuna, too). "What are you two doing?" she shouted.

Immediately Tuna grabbed his Swiss Army Knife (sold at 23rd-century time-travel stores everywhere) and closed the blade. The holographic video game disappeared. No more spacecraft, no more Bruce Bruiseabone, and no more irritating music. The fancy starship had changed back into a dusty attic.

"Hey," Herby complained, "I was really getting into that song."

He got a frown from the female—a seventh-grade girl better known as Thelma Jean Finkelstein (TJ to her friends—all four of them, if you count her gold-fish and hamster). She'd just moved from Missouri to Malibu, California (which explains why she had only four friends). If that wasn't bad enough, she had become the history project of Herby and Tuna, a couple of goofball teenagers from the 23rd century who'd traveled back in time to do a school report on her. Apparently she was going to grow up to become somebody important (if she survived junior high).

Unfortunately, the guys' time-travel pod had run out of fuel and they were stuck here.

Unfortunatelier (don't try that word in English class), TJ was the only one who could see them.

Unfortunateliest (the same goes for that word), people could still hear them.

"I told you," she whispered, "no video games after nine o'clock."

"We were just practicing." Herby flipped aside his surfer bangs and flexed his muscles. (He was always flexing his muscles to try to impress TJ.)

Tuna explained, "We need to be prepared in case Bruce Bruiseabone reappears."

"I thought he went back to the 23rd century," TJ said.

"He did," Herby agreed as he spotted a tiny fly buzzing around the room.

Tuna continued. "However, there's no telling when he'll show up again to torment us."

"Or—" Herby lowered his voice and watched the fly buzz toward the attic window—"what form he'll take when he does."

"Listen, guys," TJ said. "You can practice all you want when I'm at school and nobody's home."

"How can we protect you at school if we're practicing at home?" Tuna asked.

"My point exactly," TJ said. "I've told you a hundred times I don't want you following me." She paused to watch Herby tiptoe toward the window.

"Understood," Tuna said. "However—"

"AHHHHHHH!"

He was interrupted by the sound of Herby leaping at the fly. But Herby's leaper was a little lame and he was unable to stop at the window. Instead, he sort of

CRASH! BREAK!

tinkle-tinkle-tinkle

leaped through the glass and

roll, roll, roll

"Ouch! Ouch! ouch!"

tumbled down the roof until he

THUD

"Oooff!"

landed in the flower bed.

Tuna and TJ raced to the window.

"Herby, are you all right?" TJ cried.

"Wuaff mwabom!" Herby replied (which is the best anyone can reply with a mouthful of geraniums).

"What?"

"Mwi maid (*spit-spit*) false alarm," he finally shouted. He held out his hand and revealed one very squashed fly. "It wasn't Bruce after all!"

"Excellent news," Tuna shouted.

Of course it would have been more excellent if TJ's father wasn't shouting from downstairs, "What's going on up there? TJ, are you okay?"

Luckily, Tuna had an answer for everything. (The answer was usually wrong, but he always had one.) Without a word, he pulled open the Reverse Beam Blade of his Swiss Army Knife and

RaaAapha . . .
Reeeepha . . . Riiiipha . . .

BOING-oing-oing-oing-oing!

everything

"!FFOoo"

DUHT

that had happened

"!hcuO !hcuO !hcuO"
llor, llor, llor

was put into

elknit-elknit-elknit

!kaeRB !HSARC

reverse, until

"!HHHHHHHA"

Herby was back in the attic having the conversation about not following TJ to school.

Not that TJ was surprised. It was just another average, run-of-the-mill evening for TJ Finkelstein and her time stumblers.

* * * * *

TJ climbed down the attic steps and headed toward her bedroom. As she passed Violet's door, she saw that her middle sister still had the lights on. No surprise there. Violet always had her lights on. How else could she read 50 books a day, be president of every club in her school, and become dictator of the world before she was 16?

TJ pushed open the door to see Violet standing on a ladder. She was writing numbers on a big thermometer chart that stretched up to the ceiling.

"What are you doing?" TJ asked.

Violet answered without turning. "I'm checking to see how much more money I need to earn for Daddy's gift."

"Gift?" TJ asked. "For what?"

"Christmas. It's only 6 days, 2 hours, 6 minutes, and 46 seconds from now." (Violet liked to be precise.)

"No way!" TJ cried in alarm. "It can't be!"

"You're right." Violet rechecked her watch. "It is now 6 days, 2 hours, 6 minutes, and 41 seconds." (See what I mean?)

TJ couldn't believe it. She'd been so caught up in all her junior-high migraine makers that she hadn't even noticed it was December. It would have helped to have a few clues . . . like maybe a little less sunshine or the temperature dropping below 70 degrees. Still, if she'd been paying attention, she'd have noticed that the beach babes had changed from SPF 69 to SPF 41.

"I'm getting him an 82-inch plasma TV and installing it right in his bedroom," Violet said snootily. Violet didn't try to sound snooty; it just came naturally. "What are you getting him?"

"Something better than that," TJ said. TJ didn't try to compete with her sister . . . it just came naturally.

"Yeah?" Violet asked. "Like what?"

"Like . . . well, uh . . . it's a surprise!"

"Right," Violet snorted and went back to coloring her money thermometer.

"What? You don't think I can give Daddy a better gift than you?" TJ asked.

"Actually," Violet said, "I don't think you can do anything better than me."

TJ could feel her insides churning. She knew it would do no good to argue with her sister. Violet always thought she was right. To make matters worse, Violet always *was* right. (Well, except that one time when she thought she was wrong.) But she couldn't help saying, "Oh yeah?"

Violet gave no answer.

TJ pushed up her glasses and repeated, "Oh yeah?"

"Listen," Violet said, "don't take it personally. It's in our DNA. I got all of Mom's and Dad's brains and you got all of . . . all of . . . Well, I'm sure you got something. I mean it's not like you were adopted." She hesitated, then turned to TJ. "Were you?"

If TJ was mad before, she was outraged now. So outraged that she returned to her favorite argument. "Oh yeah?"

Violet sighed. "Haven't we already had this discussion?"

TJ wanted to fire back with a classy put-down, but somehow she knew another "oh yeah" wouldn't do the trick.

"Guys?"

They both turned to see their youngest sister,

Dorie, standing in the doorway. She was as cute as a button and almost as small.

"Can I borrow some markers?"

"Hey, Squid," TJ said. "Why are you out of bed?"

"I'm working on Daddy's Christmas gift."

"You too?" TJ groaned.

"Uh-huh," Dorie said. "I'm making him a tie clasp." Her face beamed with excitement. "I already found the clothespin. Now I just need to color it with markers."

"You're giving Dad a clothespin for Christmas?" TJ asked.

Dorie shook her head. "No. I'm giving him a clothespin *colored with markers* for Christmas."

"I see." TJ smiled. She always smiled when she talked with Dorie. Of course she tried to hide it. After all, Dorie was a younger sister, and younger sisters are supposed to irritate older sisters. (It's like a law or something.) So TJ just tousled Dorie's hair and said, "Let's head to my room to see if I have any."

"Yippee!" Dorie said as she skipped into the hallway.

But even as they headed toward her room, TJ's mind raced back to Dad. She had to get him something. Granted, she had no money, but somehow the gift had to be bigger and better than Violet ever dreamed.

Unfortunately, some dreams turn into nightmares—especially with help from the 23rd century.

CHAPTER TWO

'Tis the Season to Be Greedy

TIME TRAVEL LOG:
Malibu, California, December 19

Begin Transmission:
Subject applied for first job. A gonzo success
thanks to Tuna's incredibly smart brain, my
incredibly good looks, and our incredible
incredibleness.

End Transmission

All night long, TJ tossed and turned, worrying
about what gift to get Dad. Finally she had her
solution: a nice, big wad of cash . . . exactly one

dollar more than the cost of Violet's big-screen TV. There *was* the slight problem of being totally broke, but she could get an after-school job. After all, it was Christmastime. Plenty of stores needed help at Christmas.

Now it's true, somewhere in the back of her mind, there was a whisper that Christmas just might be more than gifts and money. But the next day, as she headed down the school hallway with Naomi Simpletwirp, it was quickly forgotten.

"Isn't this (*click-clack*) something?" Naomi said.

The *click-clack* came from the breath mint Naomi chewed. (Naomi lived in constant fear of bad breath.) And the *something* she spoke of was the student lockers—each and every one decorated to the max for Christmas.

"Wow" was all TJ could say.

"Yeah (*clack-click*), it's a tradition around here. Everyone tries to beat everyone else for the best-decorated locker."

TJ nodded as she noticed a techno geek's locker to their left. Besides the standard flashing lights (in perfect sync to "Jingle Bells"), the entire locker door had been replaced by a 3D video panel of Santa Claus

Ho-HO-Ho-ing

his heart out in THX surround sound.

Next to this was some goth chick's locker. It was draped in black velvet, covered in dripping red paint (at least TJ hoped it was paint), and had almost as many rivets punched into the door as the girl had in her ears—arranged, of course, to look like a Christmas tree.

"This is amazing," TJ said as she ducked a remote-controlled sleigh and reindeer flying overhead. "You guys really go all out."

"Sure do," Naomi said. She finished off her breath mint and dug into her purse for breath spray. "Christmas is like a major religion here."

TJ was surprised. *Religion* was not exactly a word she associated with the kids of Malibu Junior High. "Are you sure about that?" she asked.

"Sure, I'm sure," Naomi said as they passed a locker with a snowman made from real snow in front of it. "Why do you ask?"

"I don't see any religious decorations," TJ said. "You know, like baby Jesus in the manger or the three wise men or—?"

"Who would buy that stuff?"

"Buy?" TJ asked.

"If nobody buys it, what's it got to do with Christmas?"

TJ frowned. There had to be an answer there, somewhere, but before she could find it, Naomi changed subjects. "So what do you think Doug is going to get me?"

"I don't know," TJ said as they passed a Christmas tree with giant glass ornaments shaped like diamonds (at least she thought they were glass).

"Well, it better be something expensive," Naomi said as she gave up on the breath spray and began searching for a toothbrush and toothpaste. "*Real* expensive."

"Why expensive?" TJ asked.

"*Hello?* Because it's Christmas."

TJ nodded, once again remembering how broke she was and how she had to find work. "Listen," she asked, "you don't know someplace I can get a job, do you?"

"What do you need a job for?"

"Extra money."

"Just use your credit card."

TJ looked at her friend and blinked. "You have your own credit card?"

"*Hello?*" Naomi said. "This is Malibu, California."

Of course; what was she thinking? "But what if I, you know, don't have one yet? Any idea how I could get some real money?"

"Real money?" Naomi scowled. The concept was obviously new to her. "Well . . . there's Bags Fifth Avenue department store. They always hire people for the holidays."

"Fantastic," TJ said as they stepped around a miniature ice rink, complete with mechanical skating penguins (at least she thought they were mechanical). "Bags Fifth Avenue. I'll go there right after school."

* * * * *

"Hm, what an interesting idea," Hesper Breakahart said as she munched on her half stick of celery.

"Oh yes, very interesting," all the Hesper wannabes echoed as they munched on their own half sticks of celery.

Chad Steel looked across the lunch table in stunned silence. Normally the only ideas his girlfriend thought were interesting were her own. But for some reason, she actually thought *he* might have one.

"So, tell me more." Hesper munched.

"That's right; tell us more." Her wannabes munched.

Chad explained, "Every Christmas Eve my church goes out to the homeless and serves them Christmas dinner. This year I thought maybe you could join us. You know, as a TV celebrity, you might draw attention to the cause."

Hesper frowned. "Homeless people, you say?"

"Right."

"Will they bathe first?"

"Yes," her wannabes asked, "will they bathe?"

"I'm not sure," Chad said.

"Hm," Hesper replied.

"Hm," her wannabes said.

Then, before Chad could explain how important her presence might be, Hesper's face lit up. "Well, I think that's a super fantastic idea." Turning to the girls, she asked, "Don't you?"

"Oh yes. Super fantastic."

Chad was both pleased and alarmed. Pleased because Hesper had agreed to something that hadn't been her idea. Alarmed because Hesper never did anything for others—unless it made her the center of attention. (She not only liked being the star of her own TV show; she liked being the star of everyone's lives.)

Still, people could change, couldn't they? Besides, how could spending Christmas Eve feeding the

homeless possibly turn into something only about
Hesper?

But even as Chad thought that thought, he
thought that thinking that thought might be a little
thoughtless.

TRANSLATION: He should have known
better.

* * * * *

After school, TJ headed to Bags Fifth Avenue to
apply for a job. She'd already swung by Dad's office
to get written permission from him, and now she was
ready to go to work. The only problem was, so were
3,407 other people. (Well, maybe not that many,
but close.) In fact, when she entered the employees'
lounge, she counted at least six other people . . . all
on their best behavior, wearing their best clothes, and
sporting perfect white smiles.

(What is it with Californians and perfect white
smiles?)

Anyway, TJ grabbed an application form and had
started filling it out when a large woman (at least
she thought it was a woman) entered the room. TJ
guessed her to be either the store's assistant manager,

a Marine corps drill sergeant, or the star of the next King Kong movie. And she had some sort of weird accent.

"All right," the manager/sergeant/ape bellowed, "lizten up!"

Everyone smiled their perfect smiles a little more perfectly.

"We've only got one opening left, for zee pozition of Zanta'z helper. I am not wazting time interviewing each of you. Inztead, you will anzwer my queztionz here and now."

"Cool," TJ heard a voice beside her say.

She turned to see Herby floating cross-legged to her right. "Oh no," she groaned.

"Oh yes," Tuna said, floating at her other side.

"Guys," she whispered, "why are you here?"

Tuna explained, "We've come to assist you in securing the job you want."

Herby added, "Even though your reasons are majorly zworked."

"I told you I wanted to do stuff on my own," TJ whispered.

"All right!" the manager bellowed. "I want everyone on zeir feet."

Everyone rose and stood in a row . . . while Herby reached for the Swiss Army Knife.

"Herby," TJ hissed.

"Quiet!" the manager barked.

TJ watched from the corner of her eye as Herby opened a blade she had never seen before.

"You!" The woman pointed at the first girl—a pretty redhead in her late teens. "What'z your name?"

The girl cleared her throat and cranked up her smile. As she did, TJ heard the knife's blade begin to quietly

hummmm . . .

A faint blue light glowed around it and quickly spread throughout the room.

"Herby . . . ," she whispered.

"Don't worry, Your Dude-ness. It's just an old-fashioned Truth Glow."

"A what?"

Before he could respond, the redhead answered, "My name is Julie Stealublind."

The assistant manager leaned into her face. "Why are you qualified for zee job?"

"Because I'm a great shoplifter," the girl said. "I'll steal all kinds of stuff and sell it on eekBay." She threw her hands over her mouth in astonishment.

"You zink zat's funny?" the manager demanded.

"Oh no, ma'am, it's not funny—it's the truth."
The girl's eyes widened in horror as she continued
talking. "I do this every year." Desperately, she tried
to close her mouth, but it just kept on moving. "Last
Christmas I made over a thousand dollars by ripping
off the drugstore down the street. And the year
before that, it was the bookstore around the corner.
And the year before that—"

"Zilence!" the manager roared.

The girl came to a stop. She gave the manager
a pathetic little shrug, followed by a pathetic little
smile.

The manager slowly raised her hand and pointed
toward the door. "Out."

The girl nodded, grabbed her stuff, and raced for
the exit.

"Pretty outloopish, huh?" Herby whispered.

"What about you?" the manager shouted at the
next person. He was a high school kid whose arms
sported more ink than the *L.A. Times*.

"I'm here to check out the babes," he answered.
"You know, get their phone numbers and stuff."
He stopped, as shocked at what he'd said as the
redhead.

"Get out!" the manager ordered.

He turned for the door, shaking his head in confusion.

Tuna whispered, "This is working out rather nicely, wouldn't you agree?"

TJ had no answer. She could only stare as the assistant manager moved to the next in line— a blonde beauty queen.

"And what about you, cupcake?" the manager sneered. "You got any zecretz you feel like zharing?"

The girl opened her mouth but did not speak.

"What'z wrong?"

"I, uh, er . . ."

"Zpit it out."

"I'm sorry; it's just that . . . I've never seen anyone quite as ugly as you." She clamped her hands over her mouth but still managed to say, "Though I saw a Bigfoot drawing on the Discovery Channel once that reminds me of—"

"Next!"

A college student with enough grease in his hair to start a Jiffy Lube answered, "I'm looking for a job where I can slack without getting caught and—"

"Next!"

An older man replied, "My parole officer said this would be a good—"

"Next!"

A middle-aged woman answered, "I've got a crush on the store's Santa Claus and—"

"Next!"

TJ glanced around and took a deep breath. There was no next, next to her. She was the last one there.

The manager leaned in and snarled, "And what are your qualificationz?"

TJ cleared her throat.

"Well?"

Before she could stop herself, the words spilled out. "I'm a hard worker, honest, and very considerate of people."

The manager leaned closer, suspiciously eyeing her.

"And I really don't think you're ugly."

The manager continued staring.

TJ swallowed. "Well, not ugly enough to be on the Discovery Channel."

The manager folded her arms.

TJ fidgeted, grateful the woman didn't ask her what she thought of her breath.

"And why do you want zee job?" the manager asked.

"I really need the money so I can give it to my dad, 'cause he really deserves it, and my sister Violet, she—"

"All right," the woman said.

"—can really be a pain, and, I mean, I love her and everything, but she's planning on getting him this real expensive—"

"I zaid, all right."

"—big-screen TV and I want to give him something even better so—"

"ZTOP!"

TJ clamped her mouth shut.

The assistant manager paused a long moment before finally speaking. "All right, you've got zee job."

"I do?" TJ croaked.

"Go down to zee fitting room and get your elf coztume."

"What . . . now?"

"Do you want zee job or not?"

"Yes, ma'am. Like I said, my sister is buying him this—"

"Go."

"—very expensive—"

"GO!"

"Yes, ma'am. Thank you very much." TJ turned to gather her things. "I promise you won't be disappointed."

And she was right. The woman would not be disappointed. Totally astonished, yes. Completely horrified, absolutely. But disappointed, no. That was far too mild a word for what was about to happen.

CHAPTER THREE

Zmile and Zay Cheeze!

TIME TRAVEL LOG:

Malibu, California, December 19–supplemental

Begin Transmission:

Subject learning the joys of work. Still refuses our companionship. Reasons unknown as I actually showered this morning. Perhaps tomorrow I'll try using soap.

End Transmission

After putting on an elf costume that was baggy in all the wrong places and tight in all the others (although the floppy hat with the white ball on top was cool),

TJ headed into the store's lobby to begin work as Santa's helper. They'd decorated the area to look like a mountain forest, complete with rocks, fake trees, and fir branches around the floor.

The good news was TJ had finally convinced Tuna and Herby to go home and leave her alone.

The bad news was TJ had finally convinced Tuna and Herby to go home and leave her alone.

Actually, the job was simple enough. She just had to make sure the kids sitting on Santa's lap smiled when their pictures were taken.

For the older kids, this meant something complicated like standing behind the photographer and saying, "Smile!"

For the younger kids, she had a bright pink dinosaur toy that

Squeak squeak Squeak-ed

when she squeezed it. (A real sidesplitter if you're four years old.)

But for the youngest children . . . well, that's where she could have used some 23rd-century help. Because little Jimmie Johnson was definitely not in the mood to grin.

"Okay, smile!" TJ said.

Little Jimmie Johnson began to cry.

TJ grabbed the pink dinosaur and

Squeak squeak Squeak-ed

it.

Little Jimmie Johnson began to wail.

"Okay," TJ said, trying to think of a solution. "Hey, check out my funny face!" She stuck out her tongue and crossed her eyes.

Little Jimmie Johnson looked at her, blinked, then screamed his lungs out.

Unfortunately, Santa wasn't so helpful either. "Shut up," he growled at the child. And when Jimmie didn't feel like shutting up, Santa tried a more sensitive approach by yelling, "Keep your yap shut or I'll *really* give you something to cry about!" (It's not that Santa didn't have feelings for children. He had plenty. It's just that none of them were good.)

Glaring at TJ, he yelled, "Do something!"

"Right." TJ's mind raced until she had another solution. She began jumping up and down while making funny

"BUGGALA . . . BUGGALA . . . BUGGALA!"

sounds.

That nearly did the trick. Little Jimmie grew quiet for almost a second.

Almost.

TJ shouted louder. She jumped higher . . . which made the little ball on the end of her elf hat begin to

boink boink boink

her in the face. This added feature should have sent Jimmie into hysterical fits.

Unfortunately, he was too busy screaming to notice.

Next, TJ added waving both of her arms to the routine. And we're not talking a little waving. We're talking out-of-control-airplane-propeller waving.

Jimmie cranked up the volume from earhurting to earsplitting. (I don't want to say he was loud, but the cars outside were pulling over for what they thought was an approaching fire truck.)

"Do something!" Santa shouted at TJ.

"I'm (*jump jump jump*) try(*wave wave wave*)ing!"
TJ yelled as her little white ball kept

boink boink boink-ing

her in the face and she kept

**"BUGGALA . . . BUGGALA . . .
BUGGALA!"-ing**

"WELL, TRY HARDER!" Santa shouted.
She shouted back, "O—

jump jump jump

wave wave wave

boink boink boink

**BUGGALA . . . BUGGALA . . .
BUGGALA!**

"—KAY!"

But nothing worked. Until Santa, being the seasoned professional he was, grabbed Jimmie by the shoulders, spun him around, and shouted into his face. "STOP IT, YOU LITTLE BRAT!"

The good news was Jimmie Johnson immediately stopped screaming.

The bad news was Jimmie Johnson passed out in fear.

The baddest news was Jimmie Johnson's mother (better known as Mrs. Johnson) replaced her son's screaming with her own: **"WHAT HAVE YOU DONE TO MY BABY?"**

(I guess we know where her baby got his lung power.)

And the fun and games weren't exactly over. . . .

Thanks to Jimmie's screaming, Santa's yelling, and Mommy's shouting, every child in line was crying.

"WILL YOU DO SOMETHING?!" Santa yelled at TJ.

With no other plan, TJ grabbed the pink dinosaur and raced to the children,

Squeak squeak Squeak-ing

jump jump jump-ing

wave *wave* **wave**-ing

boink **boink** **boink**-ing

and of course,

"BUGGALA . . . BUGGALA . . . BUGGALA!"-ing

her heart out as she ran up and down the line
making goofy faces.

To be honest, she didn't know if it would work.
And when she reached the end of the line, she didn't
much care. Because there, holding the hand of his
terrified little cousin, stood Chad Steel.

Chad Steel . . . whose name TJ had scrawled all
over the inside of her notebook.

Chad Steel . . . who already thought TJ belonged
in a mental hospital.

Chad Steel . . . who

Squeak *squeak* **Squeak**

jump jump **jump**

wave wave wave

boink boink boink

**"BUGGALA . . . BUGGALA . . .
BUGGALA!"**

was watching TJ with a sad little smile—the type you give crazy people on the street or prisoners on their way to being executed.

* * * * *

It was 8:00 p.m. when TJ staggered home from work and opened the front door.

"Hey, sport," Dad said as he looked up from the TV remote, which he'd been trying to figure out since 2008.

"TJ!" Dorie cried as she raced from the Christmas tree she was trying to decorate near the stairs.

"No, Squid, don't!" But TJ's warning was too late. The little girl leaped into her arms, practically knocking her over.

Meanwhile, Violet sat quietly in the corner, working on her laptop—no doubt selling stocks that would pay for Dad's big-screen TV.

But something was wrong. TJ could tell instantly. Why else would all of them be together in the same room at the same time? It's not that they didn't spend time together, but for them, "quality family time" usually just meant passing each other on their way to the bathroom in the morning.

Dad did his best to smile, but it was more of a grimace—which meant he either had terrible news or a bad case of indigestion. "Sweetheart, you better sit down."

So much for the indigestion.

Filled with dread, TJ headed for the sofa. The last time they'd had a meeting like this was when he told them Mom was sick. "What happened?" she asked. "What's wrong?"

Once again Dad tried to smile . . . and once again he didn't quite succeed.

TJ braced herself for the worst as Dorie plopped down beside her and Violet actually paused from typing.

He cleared his throat and began. "Remember I was telling you how my company has been in bad shape the past few months?"

TJ nodded.

"Well . . ." He took a deep breath. "In order to cut back expenses, they had to let me go."

"Let you go where?" Dorie asked.

Dad smiled. For real this time. "It means I was fired, honey."

"You lost your job?" TJ croaked.

"Only for a little while. They promise to rehire me just as soon as things get better."

"So you're, like, on a vacation," Dorie said.

"Sort of, yes."

"Cool."

Finally Violet spoke up. "But with no salary, no health benefits, and unemployment pay amounting to a fraction of your current gross income."

All three looked at Violet like she was speaking a foreign language.

Dad slowly nodded. "That's right."

"Is that a good or bad thing?" Dorie asked.

Dad took another breath. "Actually, both. It means Christmas gifts are going to be real slim this year."

Silence filled the room.

"But—" he returned to his smile—"it also means we'll be able to focus on more important things, like spending time with one another."

"So you're spending more time with us?" Dorie said as she hopped off the sofa and crawled onto his lap.

"That's right," Dad said. He pulled her closer. "I'm going to have all sorts of time."

"But you're still going to let us do the cooking, right?" Violet asked in alarm.

"Oh, I don't know. With all my free time, I might be able—"

"No, Dad, please," TJ said.

"No offense," Violet explained, "but if they had an event in the Olympics for awful cooking—"

TJ finished her thought. "You'd bring home the gold every time."

"And the silver and bronze," Violet said.

"Please, Daddy," Dorie begged. "Please don't cook for us."

"For the good of your family," TJ said.

"For the good of the human race," Violet added.

"All right, all right." He laughed. "I promise, I will not cook."

"And that includes trying to boil water," TJ said.

Dorie agreed. "I hate burnt water."

He chuckled. "I won't even boil water."

The mood in the room lightened and Dad gave Dorie another hug. "We may not have presents this year, but we'll have each other."

"And that's what really counts," Dorie said, hugging him back.

Dad held her close. "And that's what really counts."

Everyone seemed to agree . . . or at least

pretended to. But even as they nodded, Violet
returned to her typing, working all the more fever-
ishly. And TJ knew what that meant. Now, more
than ever, Violet was going to get Dad that big-
screen TV. Which meant now, more than ever,
TJ would have to earn enough money to beat her.

CHAPTER FOUR

Shopping Spree...
23rd-Century Style

TIME TRAVEL LOG:

Malibu, California, December 19–supplemental
of supplemental

Begin Transmission:

*Invited subject to go shopping. Hoped to make a
sale for Uncle Dorkel. But alas and alack (whatever
that means), there's no pleasing her. 21st-century
chicks can be so picky.*

End Transmission

TJ opened the door to her room and sighed. You'd
sigh too if you spotted two goofballs from the 23rd
century floating above your desk.

"Hey there, Your Dude-ness." Herby grinned, sucking in his stomach and doing his usual failure at looking buff. "You miss us?"

If TJ rolled her eyes any harder, she would have sprained them.

"How was your first day at work?" Tuna asked.

She plopped down on the bed and stared at the ceiling. "You're telling me you didn't drop by to spy on me?"

"Of course not," Tuna said.

She looked at him.

"Well, not *all* the time."

She gave another weary sigh. "Why don't you guys head up to your attic and we'll talk tomorrow. I'm really wiped out."

"Actually, that's what we want to talk with you about," Tuna said. "We've concluded that you are placing far too much emphasis on the material aspects of the holiday season."

"In English, please?" TJ asked.

Herby translated: "Christmas is way more than spending outloopish bucks and getting gonzo gifts."

She sighed again and looked at the ceiling. "Not around here it isn't."

Tuna argued, "But as a future leader, who will one day save the planet—"

"And bring back the hula hoop," Herby added.

"—you must ignore what others say and do the right thing," Tuna explained. "In this case, it is experiencing the true nature of Christmas."

"You mean like 'Away in a Manger' and 'Silent Night' and all that?" TJ asked.

"If 'all that' includes loving others as God loves them, then yes."

"But giving cool gifts shows love," TJ said.

"Sometimes," Tuna agreed.

"But there are even more fantabulouser ways," Herby said.

TJ closed her eyes. "Well, giving Dad a big wad of cash and beating out Violet is going to be my way." Suddenly she had an idea and sat up. "Unless you guys could whip up something with that fancy knife of yours."

Tuna stiffened. "The 23rd-century Swiss Army Knife doesn't *whip up* things."

"Right," TJ snorted, "except trouble for yours truly."

"There is absolutely no blade on that knife that manufactures gifts."

"Except . . . ," Herby said, thinking deeply (obviously a new experience for him), "you could buy something really groovy from the future and have it FedEx-ed back to you."

"Herby!" Tuna warned.

"Hey, I'm just trying to help."

"You're just trying to get her to like you," Tuna argued.

"What makes you say that?" Herby said, sucking in his gut a little more and flexing his arms a little bigger.

But TJ barely noticed. "You're telling me I can buy stuff from the future for my dad? And that your Swiss Army Knife can ship it back to me?"

"Yes!" Herby said at the same time Tuna was saying, "No!"

"Really?" she asked.

More "Yes!"es and "No!"s (with an extra "Absolutely not" thrown in by Tuna).

"Ah, come on," TJ said. She rose from the bed and approached Tuna. "That would be so cool."

He looked away.

"Please?"

He folded his arms, but she could tell he was already starting to weaken.

"Pretty please . . ."

"It goes entirely against the character you should be developing for the future."

"Just this once?" She batted her eyes, trying to look sweet and innocent.

Tuna cleared his throat and faced his partner . . .
who was also batting his eyes and looking sweet and
innocent.

"Please?" TJ repeated.

Tuna swallowed uneasily.

"Just this once?"

"Well . . ." He hesitated. "Okay, but just once."

"All right!" TJ cried.

"Wazferk!" Herby shouted as he high-fived her.
Then, reaching into his pocket for the knife, Herby
opened a new blade and

toga-oga-oga-oga-oga . . .

a bright orange light filled the room.

"So what hobbies does your father enjoy?" Tuna
asked.

"Besides burning our meals and trying to figure
out the remote?" TJ said.

"Correct."

"Well, he likes to read books."

"Don't tell us, Your Dude-ness," Herby said,
holding out the knife. "Talk to the blade."

TJ leaned toward the knife and said, "Books."

Suddenly

fwwa**aark** ...
POP!

a thousand different bottles of pills floated around her—small, big, clear, amber.

"What's this?" she said. "He likes books, not medicine."

"They're books," Herby said.

"They're pills," she argued.

"Exactly," Tuna agreed.

"How do you read a pill?"

"You don't read pills," Herby said. "You swallow them."

"By prescription only," Tuna clarified. "That's how 23rd-century citizens get information from books."

TJ frowned and reached for the nearest bottle as it floated by. She read the label. *The Adventures of Huckleberry Finn.* You mean if I take this pill, I'll have all the information that's in the book?"

"Once you digest it, it goes straight to your brain."

TJ nodded, thinking how lucky 23rd-century students would be. Forget school; just go to the doctor and get a prescription. "But . . . what about the actual reading? Dad likes to read."

"Reading?" Tuna scoffed. "That's so 21st-century."

"But it's what he likes."

"Sorry." Herby shrugged.

"How 'bout travel?" Tuna asked. "Does he enjoy traveling?"

"We went to Detroit once, for a convention."

"Not exactly what I meant." Turning to the blade, Tuna spoke the word *vacation*, and immediately

fwwa**aark** . . .

POP!

a giant model of a planet was floating in TJ's room. (At least she hoped it was model.)

"What's that?" she asked.

"You can buy your father his own private planet," Tuna said.

"Perfect for those times he wants to get away," Herby explained.

"Really?" TJ asked in growing excitement.

"Absolutely," Tuna said. "Though it will involve putting him into hyperfreeze for the several hundred years it will take to travel to his destination. However—"

TJ shook her head. "What else do you have?"

"Does he like pets?" Herby asked.

"Sure, we got the cat, the dog, my hamster, my goldfish—"

"No, I'm talking unique pets."

TJ knew she shouldn't ask the question (especially with these guys), but she couldn't help herself. "What do you mean . . . *unique?*"

As an answer, Herby spoke into the blade: "Uncle Dorkel's Pet Store." And suddenly

fwwaaark . . .

POP!

scurrying around her room were a couple of very strange animals. And we're not talking your average strange (even for TJ's life). We're talking your stranger than strange.

"What are they?" TJ cried in alarm.

"Design-a-Pets," Herby said proudly. "My uncle owns the store."

"Really?" TJ asked. She reached down and caught

what looked like a tiny chow chow—except for the part about its jumping only on back legs and having a cute little pouch in its tummy. "What's this?"

"A miniature kanga-chow," Tuna said. "Quite popular among the rich and famous."

"Why's that?"

"Not only do their owners keep them in their purses, but they can use their little pouches to hold their makeup."

TJ sighed. "That's not exactly Dad's style." She set the kanga-chow down and watched it hop off. Not far away she spotted something that resembled a cat, except it walked on two legs and was holding a banana. "What's that?" she asked.

"A chimpanz-kitty," Herby said.

TJ watched as it jumped up to her chair and then onto her desk, where it picked up a pencil and examined it.

Tuna explained, "It's the perfect pet for those who enjoy cats but want them to empty their own litter box."

TJ raised an eyebrow. "How much does it cost?"

Herby reached for the chimpanz-kitty and read the tag on its collar. "Just $34.95."

"That's it?"

"Plus shipping and handling."

"And how much is that?"

"One, maybe two billion."

"Dollars?" TJ choked.

"Give or take a million."

"That's terrible!" TJ said.

"Well, you have to figure for inflation."

"And two hundred years is an outloopish distance to travel," Herby said.

"Sorry, guys. That's a little out of my range. I think I better stick to Plan A. With Dad being out of work and everything, the more money I can give to him, the better."

"But, Your Dude-ness, we just explained—"

"I know what you explained," she said as she crossed to her door and opened it. "I also know what I've decided."

"But—"

"Good night, guys." She motioned to the hallway. "I'll see you in the morning."

Reluctantly, they nodded and floated toward the door.

"And take your pals with you."

"What if Uncle Dorkel dropped the price to $29.95?" Herby asked.

"Plus shipping and handling?" TJ asked.

He shrugged.

"Good night."

"How 'bout two for the price of one?"

"Good night, guys."

"Good night," they muttered as they floated out of the room and down the hallway.

She called after them, "Herby? The animals?"

He pulled out the knife, pressed the blade, and

fwwa**aark** . . .

POP!

everything was gone.

TJ closed the door, shaking her head. She was grateful to finally be alone . . . well, except for the empty banana peel left by a 23rd-century chimpanz-kitty.

CHAPTER FIVE

Popcorn and Pop Stars

TIME TRAVEL LOG:

Malibu, California, December 20

Begin Transmission:
Tuna and I are going way overboard to be more
than helpful. For some unknown reason, this makes
subject way more ungrateful. Guess we'll have to try
way more harder.

End Transmission

The next day, after school, Chad went with Hesper
to see her manager, Bernie Makeabuck. Together
they sat on his rich Beverly Hills sofa in his rich

Beverly Hills office, talking about feeding the not-so-rich hungry.

Mr. Makeabuck, who was somewhere between fifty and a hundred (it was hard to tell with all the plastic surgery and hair transplants), was pacing back and forth in his office. He was dressed, tatted, and pierced like some MTV host.

"That's absolutely fantastic, babe!" he said.

"Really?" Chad asked. "You think it's good idea?"

"You bet! Especially if you wear your bikini."

Chad blinked. "Excuse me?"

"You know, the one that makes all the guys go crazy."

Chad traded uneasy looks with Hesper, who would have traded uneasy looks with Chad if she hadn't been reading the latest article about herself in *Teen Wannabe*.

Mr. Makeabuck smiled. "So lay a big kiss on me and we got a deal."

Chad frowned. "I'm sorry; that's not exactly what—"

The manager turned to Chad, motioning to the Bluetooth in his ear. Apparently one conversation wasn't enough for Mr. Makeabuck. He had two going—one with Chad, one on his cell phone—until his desk phone rang and he picked it up to start a third. "What's up?"

As Mr. Makeabuck listened, he pointed to Chad and mouthed the words *Talk to me.*

Chad cleared his throat and tried again. "I was saying, if Hesper could join my church in feeding the homeless on Christmas Eve—"

"Fantastic! Yes! Absolutely brilliant!"

Chad hesitated, unsure who Mr. Makeabuck was talking to until the manager nodded for him to continue.

He coughed nervously. "We figured if Hesper joined us, then more people would pay attention to the problems of the homeless and—"

Mr. Makeabuck clapped. "We'll ship them all off to Afghanistan."

"The homeless?" Chad asked.

Mr. Makeabuck motioned to his phone and continued talking into it. "Absolutely, having the band play for our soldiers is brilliant. Call me back 911 with the 411! Love ya too, babe." He hung up and faced Chad. "Where were we?"

"I was saying—"

The phone rang again.

"Hold that thought." Mr. Makeabuck scooped up the receiver.

Chad slumped into the couch.

Hesper looked up from her article. "So are you two having a nice talk?"

Chad motioned to Mr. Makeabuck, who was busy with his multiple conversations. "I don't think he's heard a word I've said."

"Of course not."

"Of course not?" Chad asked.

"No, silly. You have to be super rich and disgustingly famous for him to pay attention."

Chad shook his head. "Then why are we here?"

"Because *I'm* super rich and disgustingly famous."

"But—"

"Watch and learn." Suddenly Hesper's sweeter-than-sweet face turned to a sourer-than-sour expression as she screamed, "I AM NOT HAPPY!"

Mr. Makeabuck startled. His own face grew white with fear. "Got an emergency!" he shouted into the phone. "Call me and we'll do lunch!" He hung up and gave Hesper his full attention. "What's the matter, babe?"

Instantly Hesper turned on the tears. "My boyfriend (*sniff-sniff*) has a fantastic idea and you're not (*sob-sob*) even listening." (The gal was definitely Oscar material.)

"That's not true, babe," Mr. Makeabuck said as he

crossed around the desk and handed her a tissue.
"I heard every word."

Hesper gazed through her tears while making her
lip tremble and her chin quiver all at the same time.
(I told you she was good.) "You did?" she asked in
her most helpless voice.

"You bet, and I think it's fantastic. Absolutely
brilliant. It'll be the news event of the season!"

"Just the season?" Hesper sniffed.

"Of the year. Of the entire decade!" He lowered
his voice, but it quickly rose in excitement. "We'll
contact all the networks. Have them set up their
cameras. And then, when everything's set, we'll bring
you in by helicopter to greet the cheering masses."

"Oooh—" Hesper giggled—"I like that."

"Actually," Chad coughed, "that might be a little
more than I—"

"Better yet! We'll lower you down to them on
a cable!"

"Yes!" Hesper clapped. "I love it, love it, love it!"

"I can see it now." Mr. Makeabuck grew breath-
less in excitement. "Everyone is wondering, 'Where
will the food come from? Who will save the poor
and downtrodden?' And then the lights blaze on and
there you are, dropping down from the sky, like an
angel from heaven!"

"Perfect!" Hesper cried.

"In fact, we'll have the wardrobe department design a giant pair of angel wings you can flap!"

"Perfect! Perfect! Perfect!"

"We'll even hire the Los Angeles Symphony Orchestra to play the Hallelujah Chorus as you fly in!"

Hesper clapped her hands and squealed in delight as she said to Chad, "I told you he was a genius!"

Chad fidgeted. "I was thinking of just having her work beside the rest of us. You know, showing how we're all the same—just one human being helping another?"

The room grew deathly still, worse than the dinner table when you tell Mom you flunked the math quiz.

Finally Hesper choked out the words, "You want me to be like—" she shuddered—"everyone else?"

"Well, yeah," Chad said, "that's the whole point." He glanced at Mr. Makeabuck, whose jaw hung so low it rested on his desk. Then he turned back to Hesper, whose sweet, innocent expression had become a deadly death glare.

He swallowed.

More glaring.

More swallowing (except that his mouth had gone totally dry).

And then, just before Hesper leaped out of the chair to strangle him, Mr. Makeabuck broke into a chuckle. "Hey, that's great, kid." His chuckle transformed into laughter. "You got yourself a keeper here, babe. I mean this kid is funnnnn-y!"

Hesper's glare vanished as quickly as it appeared. "Yeah, he really is sweet." She gave Chad a look making it clear he better be.

Mr. Makeabuck continued laughing. "What a sense of humor. You really had us going there, kid."

"Actually, I—" Chad's voice caught and he tried again. "What I mean is—"

The desk phone rang and Mr. Makeabuck grabbed it. "Speak to me!" he demanded. Next, his Bluetooth began flashing and he answered, "What's up?" All this as he turned to Hesper and mouthed the words *Fantastic! Beautiful, babe!*

Hesper rose to her feet. "Oh, goody!"

The manager gave her a wink and continued talking into his phones.

She blew him a kiss and headed for the door.

"That's . . . it?" Chad asked as he stood to join her.

She wrapped her arm around his. "Bernie will take care of everything."

"Really?" Chad said. "I mean, he understands what

we want, right?" He turned to Mr. Makeabuck, who gave them a thumbs-up.

"Bernie's a pro. He understands everything."

"But—"

"Come on, I saw a photographer downstairs. We can't let him leave without getting some pictures of me."

"Yeah . . . sure," Chad said as she pulled him toward the door.

"Oh, this is going to be so much fun!" Hesper said. "The most special Christmas ever!"

"Yeah, special," Chad repeated. But even as they entered the hallway and headed for the elevators, he was afraid Hesper Breakahart's version of *special* might not be exactly the same as his.

* * * * *

The good news was TJ's second day at the department store was not as hard as her first. The bad news was (you guessed it) it was harder.

For starters, Santa was even crankier than yesterday. There were lots of possible reasons, so it's important we give the guy a break. I mean, maybe

—he was just having a bad day

—he wasn't taking his medication

—the FBI had just discovered he was a serial killer escaped from the local prison

Whatever the reason, Mr. Ho-Ho-Ho-and-a-Merry-Christmas-to-All had turned into Mr. I-Hate-My-Job-and-Who-Let-In-All-These-Kids?

When he wasn't screaming at the children who were screaming at him or shouting at the parents who were shouting at him, he was yelling at TJ:

"This coffee is 10 minutes old!" He spit it back into the cup. "I told you I wanted fresh!"

"But 10 minutes is—"

"Are you arguing with Santa?"

"No, sir."

"And I clearly said 4½ packets of sugar. You gave me 5!"

"Yes, sir."

"Well, don't stand there! Get me some more and make it fresh this time!"

"What about the children? I'm supposed to make them smile for their photos."

"Listen, sweetie, if Santa ain't smilin', no one's smilin'. Now get me that coffee!"

"Yes, sir."

So for the fourth time that afternoon, TJ ran to

the employees' lounge to fix the jolly old grump a cup of coffee.

"What a pain in the doo-wa," a voice said.

She looked up to see Tuna sitting on top of the snack machine. "What are you doing here?" she asked as she poured the coffee.

Tuna jerked his thumb toward the popcorn machine. "I came because he came."

"And what are *you* doing here?" she asked Herby, who had miniaturized himself to six inches and sat in a pile of fluffy kernels, munching away.

Herby jerked his thumb toward Tuna. "I came because (*munch-munch*) he came."

TJ shook her head. Sometimes it did absolutely no good talking to them. She counted the sugar packets as she began dumping them into the coffee.

"So why is this Santa dude so gur-roid?" Herby asked.

TJ carefully measured out the last half packet. "Maybe he's just having a rotten day," she said.

"Or a rotten life," Tuna suggested.

She stirred the coffee and started for the door. "I'm sure there's a reason for him being so cranky."

Tuna shook his head. "We already checked with the FBI, and there are no escaped serial killers on the loose."

TJ was stepping into the hallway when she heard a faint

Chugga-Chugga-Chugga

which, as we all know by now, is the sound 23rd-century Swiss Army Knives make when transporting 23rd-century time travelers off snack machines and out of popcorn poppers and

BLING! BLING!

into hallways beside 21st-century girls dressed up like goofy elves.

"If the dude is such a hothead," Herby said, munching on his last bite of popcorn, "I say we cool him down a bit."

"Guys," TJ whispered as they entered the lobby and moved through the crowd of shoppers.

"How do you propose we do that?" Tuna asked.

Herby answered, "Maybe he needs to visit Rudolph and all his reindeer pals."

"You'd send him to the North Pole?" Tuna asked.

"That's crazy," TJ whispered louder.

"She's right. Far too extreme," Herby agreed. "How 'bout Alaska?"

"Guys!" She was so loud that half a dozen customers turned toward her. She lowered her voice and continued. "You will not send him to the North Pole or to Alaska."

"I hear the moon is lovely this time of year," Tuna suggested.

TJ sighed loudly. "You will not send him anywhere. You will go home and you will let me—" She came to a stop. "Uh-oh."

Directly in front of them, she saw that the line for Santa had doubled in length. People were practically out in the street. And the reason? Santa had quit working and was talking on his cell phone.

"Excuse me?" a customer called from behind TJ. "Miss . . . miss?"

TJ turned and gasped. You'd gasp too if you discovered that behind you, in all of her weirdness (if you call wearing a dress made of 1,023 living flies whose bodies had been taped together but whose wings could still

buzz . . . buzZ . . . buzz . . .

weird), stood the famous pop star . . . Lady Goo-Goo.

"Are you an employee here?" the singer asked.

TJ might have nodded—she wasn't sure.

"Would you mind helping my children buy their Christmas gifts?"

TJ stood speechless.

"I'm in a rush, so if you could help out till their nanny shows up, I'd really appreciate it."

TJ glanced down and saw three rather odd-looking children. The oldest appeared to be about ten. Her hair was pulled back tight and she wore a surgical mask over her face. The next oldest was about seven. He was immersed in the latest PSP game and dressed up like a Viking, complete with a hairy vest, a furry shield strapped to his arm, and a silly-looking hat with horns sprouting from the top. Finally, there was the youngest. She was about four and a bit more normal. (If you call wearing a diving mask, complete with snorkel, normal.)

TJ looked back to Lady Goo-Goo and answered, "Um . . . er . . . uh . . ." (which wasn't much of an improvement over when she'd been speechless).

The pop star smiled. "Their nanny will be here in a few minutes. Just buy them whatever they want." Before TJ could answer, the singer stooped to give all three children a group hug. "'Cause Momma wants her babies happy and she loves them soooo much."

TJ was about to explain that she really didn't have time to be a babysitter, but she was interrupted by Santa, who bellowed, "Where's my coffee?"

She held the mug high over her head. "Right here, sir!" She started making her way through the crowd.

"Well, hurry up!"

"Coming."

"Faster, you idiot, before it gets cold!"

Out of the corner of her eye, she saw Herby pointing the blade of his Swiss Army Knife.

"Herby, no!" she cried.

Meanwhile, Santa just kept spreading his yuletide sneer. "You're one sorry excuse for an assistant, not to mention a human be—"

Unfortunately, he didn't finish his sentence. It's not that TJ enjoyed being made fun of, but anything would have been better than hearing the ever-unpopular

Chugga-Chugga-Chugga

BLING

(Which, of course, is the sound a Swiss Army Knife
makes when transporting a very cranky Santa on a
very cold trip to

"Stay cool," Herby called after him.

the North Pole.)

CHAPTER SIX

An Ideally Unideal Idea

TIME TRAVEL LOG:

Malibu, California, December 20-supplemental

Begin Transmission:

Subject making new friends . . . and they're even weirder than Tuna.

End Transmission

With Santa's visit to the land of frozen yogurt (and frozen everything else), TJ figured she had the rest of the night off. And she might have . . . if she hadn't looked down and seen Lady Goo-Goo's kids waiting to be entertained.

Actually, it wasn't that big of a deal. What had the famous singer said? Just watch them for a few minutes till the nanny showed up? No problem. TJ could handle that.

"Okay." She smiled at them. "Where would you like to go?"

The two sisters stared at her and blinked. The brother was too engrossed i his PlayStation to care.

"How 'bout the toy department?" TJ said. "The toy department sounds good, doesn't it?" She waited.

More staring and more blinking.

"All righty," she said, finally taking charge, "to the toy department we'll go. Follow me." As they started through the store, she turned to the oldest, the one who wore the surgical mask and gloves. "What's your name?" she asked.

The girl mumbled, "Mwumber mwone."

TJ leaned closer. "I'm sorry; what did you say?"

"Mwumber mwone!"

TJ frowned. "I can't understand you through the mask."

"Number One," her brother said, still focused on his game. "Her name is Number One."

It was TJ's turn to blink. "Really?"

"What else would you name your first child?" the boy said.

TJ thought of a thousand other possibilities but decided not to answer. At last they arrived at the toy department. She asked the girl, "And what would you like for Christmas, Number One?"

"Mwevrything."

"I'm sorry?" TJ said.

"Everything," the brother answered.

TJ glanced at the nearest toy display. It held about a dozen dolls. "You want all of them?" she asked in surprise. Talk about spoiled. Then again, their mother was a gazillionaire. "You want *all* these dolls?"

Number One shook her head and repeated, "Mwevrything."

TJ turned to the brother, waiting for a translation.

"Everything," the boy said without looking up. "I told you she wants *everything.*"

TJ arched an eyebrow as realization slowly sank in. "Everything?" she asked. "You want *every* toy in the department?"

The girl nodded.

"You're joking, right?"

"Does she sound like she's joking?" the brother asked.

"Well, I can't really tell," TJ said. "Here." She reached for the girl's mask. "Let me take that off so we can have a real conversa—"

"MWAUGH!" Number One screamed as she scampered behind her brother. Quickly she reached into her pocket, pulled out a can of disinfectant, and began spraying the air. "Mwerms! Mwerms! Mwerms!"

"What?" TJ asked.

"She's got a thing about germs," her brother said.

"Ah." TJ suddenly felt a little sorry for her. "She has a phobia, then."

"Whatever," the boy said, still playing his game. "If you ask me, she's just crazy."

TJ knelt to the boy's level. "And what's your name?"

"Number Too," he said. (Not only was their mother short in the creativity department, she wasn't such a great speller, either.)

"And what would *you* like for Christmas?" TJ asked.

The boy raised his Viking battle shield high and cried, "World domination!"

"I'm sorry?"

"I want to take over the world!"

"Of course you do," TJ said as she realized his older sister might not have the market cornered in craziness. She took a nervous peek at her watch. The nanny should be here any second . . . she hoped.

Finally she spoke to the youngest, who was still wearing the diver's mask and snorkel. "And what's your name, princess?"

The girl took a step backward.

"She's kinda shy," Number Too said as he returned to his game.

"She doesn't talk to strangers?" TJ asked.

"She doesn't talk to anybody," the boy said.

TJ nodded, feeling even more sympathy. This time for all three of them. They were cute kids, but they were sure messed up. "What's her name?" she asked the brother.

"Number Thuree," he said. (See what I mean about the spelling?)

TJ turned back to the girl. "And what does Number Thuree want for Christmas?"

The little sister lowered her eyes and shook her head.

TJ moved closer and smiled. "It's okay, sweetie. You can tell me."

Again she shook her head.

Finally Number Too answered. "She wants to go home and get back in the tub."

"Ah." TJ smiled. "You like taking baths? Me too. I like big, bubbly ones. Is that what you like, taking big, bubbly baths in the tub?"

The girl started to look up, then glanced back down and shook her head.

"No?" TJ asked.

"Nah," Number Too said. "She lives there."

TJ glanced at him. "Lives . . . in the tub?"

"Sleeps, eats . . . she does everything there, 24-7. Unless Bertha catches her."

"Bertha?"

"Our handler."

"You mean your nanny? The person who looks after you when your mother can't?"

"Which is like all the time."

"But your mother was just here."

"For about 30 seconds." The boy shrugged. "It's not her fault. She's too busy being famous to spend time with us. You know how it is."

TJ didn't know how it was, but the more time she spent with these three, the more she was beginning to understand.

"There you are!"

They spun around to see a fierce-looking woman who had definitely lost the art of smiling . . . if she ever had it. As she spoke, all three children stiffened in fear.

"Get your rears over here. Now!"

They immediately scrambled to her side.

The woman approached TJ, suddenly all sweetness. "I do hope they weren't too much trouble."

"Oh no." TJ smiled back. "No trouble at all."

The woman's upper lip twitched ever so slightly. "I find that rather hard to believe." Then, turning to the children, she barked, "Don't just stand there. Get in the limo!"

Without a word they ran for the door.

The nanny approached TJ and pulled a pair of tickets from her pocket. "This should cover any inconvenience they put you through. They're front-row tickets to the next Goo-Goo concert."

"No, that's okay," TJ said. "I was happy to—"

The woman shoved the tickets into TJ's hands. "Believe me, it's the least I can do to thank you for giving me a break from those brats."

"No, really—"

The nanny caught Number Thuree peeking around the corner. "What are you staring at? Get in the limo! Now!"

The little girl ducked around the corner and disappeared. Without a word the woman followed, shouting, "Move it. Let's go, let's go, let's go!"

Unsure what to say, TJ heard herself calling after them, "Merry Christmas!"

The nanny didn't answer. And as TJ watched her

disappear from sight, she felt even more sadness for the children.

But it didn't last long.

"You zere!"

She turned to see the Bags Fifth Avenue assistant manager glaring at her with the same warmth the store Santa was no doubt experiencing during his vacation up north.

"Hi." TJ smiled nervously. "Too bad about Santa." Then, trying to sound as innocent as possible, she added, "I wonder where he could have gone."

But the assistant manager was not in the mood for chitchat. She had more important things on her mind. "Come wiz me."

* * * * *

Five hours later (and still wearing her stupid elf costume), TJ dragged herself up the porch steps to her house. She was waaaay more tired than the day before, because she had worked waaaay harder than the day before, because she had worked waaaay longer than the day before, because . . .

Well, let's cut to the chase and just say that a thousand screaming kids standing in line with a thousand screaming mothers (and no Santa for them to scream at) made things a little difficult.

Things got even more difficult when the assistant manager shared her idea. Unfortunately her idea wasn't as good as TJ's idea, so it was an unideal idea but a better idea than no idea . . . ideally speaking.

TRANSLATION: The woman's idea stank.

"We need you to take mezzages for Zanta," she had said to TJ.

"What?" TJ asked.

"Juzt for tonight," the manager said confidentially as she led TJ to the front of the line.

"Juzt until tomorrow," she said officially as she stood TJ in front of Santa's throne.

"He'll be back by morning," she said assuringly as she handed TJ a pen and paper.

"At leazt I hope zo," she muttered fearfully as she disappeared into the crowd.

And so, after five hours of listening to everybody (and their mother) complaining about Santa's absence and doing her best to smile and take messages, TJ had finally ended her day and arrived home. But she'd barely reached the front door when she heard a terrifying

ROARRRr

rumble-rumble-rumble-rumble

coming from inside. She froze in fear. Her mind raced a thousand miles an hour. What could it be? A chain saw? Had someone brought a chain saw into the house?

ROARRRr

rumble-rumble-rumble-rumble

Or motorcycles? Had a gang of motorcyclists broken into her home?

Filled with panic (courtesy of all those creepy movies she'd seen), TJ shouted, "Tuna?! Herby?!"

But there was no answer. Honestly, where was a good 23rd-century time traveler when you needed one?

ROARRRR

rumble-rumble-rumble-rumble

She stared at the door. Her family was inside. Who knew what could be happening to them. Somebody had to do something. And since there was no body but TJ's body, TJ was the somebody whose body had to do it.

TRANSLATION: . . . (Never mind; No translation necessary.)

With a breath for courage and a prayer that she wouldn't die before being kissed (particularly by a handsome next-door neighbor), TJ threw open the door and leaped into the front room doing her best karate moves and shouting

"HI-YA! HOY! HA!"

She had no idea what that meant, which was okay because she had no idea how to do karate moves, either.

The good news was no one had sawed up her family's furniture (or her family), and there were no unsightly motorcycle skid marks (or bloodstains) to scrub out of the carpet.

The bad news was the noise was louder. A lot louder. And it was coming from the dining room just down the hall. TJ pressed herself flat against the wall. Her heart pounded like a jackhammer on too many cups of coffee. Ever so slowly, she began inching her way along the hall toward the dining room. As she did, the noise grew louder. And the louder it grew, the more she prayed. . . .

"Dear God, about that aardvark I made fun of in Mr. Beaker's science class? It's really not that ugly. In fact, I think it's some of your best work." (She figured if she was going to die and meet God, it wouldn't hurt to get on his good side.)

"And about Violet—I'm sorry for not treating her better. But really, you gotta admit she's awfully—"

ROARRRᴿ

rumble-rumble-rumble-rumble

"Okay, okay! She's cool, she's cool. I'll be nicer to her; I promise!"

At last she reached the end of the hallway. She paused to listen but heard nothing. Though her jack-hammer heart sounded like she'd added a couple of Red Bull drinks to those cups of coffee.

Well, it was now or never. Although she would have preferred never, she took one last breath, said one last prayer ("And please don't let them bury me in this stupid elf costume"), and leaped into the room to meet her fate.

At first, the only fate she met was the silly white ball on her elf hat bouncing into her face. She flung it aside and saw . . .

Nothing.

Well, nothing except Dad sitting in front of his computer at the dining room table with his head thrown back and

rOARRRr

rumble-rumble-rumble-rumble

snoring away.

She shook her head. Of course. Dad was a world-class snorer. But never down here in the dining room. He must have been working late on his laptop. She watched a moment as he slept. He seemed so much older than before. It was weird—Mom had died less than a year ago, but Dad looked like he'd gotten 10 years older. Maybe he had. She knew he was under a lot of pressure. Trying to keep the family together and raising three girls on his own was no picnic. Yet he was always there for them—always willing to listen, always willing to understand . . . even when they were being jerks.

As TJ watched, she felt her throat tighten with emotion. His hair was kinda messed up. Without Mom around to remind him, he never quite got it combed right. The same was true with his clothes. With nobody to fix his collars or straighten his sweaters, he always looked just a little rumpled.

Finally she whispered, "Dad?"

He gave no answer.

She walked over and gently touched him on the shoulder. "Daddy?"

He woke with a snort. "Oh, hi, TJ." He reached to the table for his glasses but couldn't find them. "When did you get home?"

"Just now," she said. "Sorry I missed dinner."

He nodded as he continued his search. "We missed you. It was Violet's turn to cook."

"Oh, then maybe I'm not sorry."

He gave her a look and she shrugged.

"Listen, you haven't seen my glasses, have you?"

"Here." TJ reached for them on his head and gently pulled them down onto his face.

"Oh." He seemed a bit embarrassed. "Thanks."

She nodded.

"You know, sweetheart, dinner is about the only time we have as a family these days."

"I know," she said. "But tonight was kind of an emergency."

He looked at her a moment. "Are you really sure you want this job?"

"I'm sure, Daddy."

"Well, all right, then. I appreciated your calling and letting me know you'd be late." He glanced at his watch. "Speaking of which, you'd better be getting to bed, young lady."

"Yeah, you're right." She started toward the hallway but stopped and turned back to him. "Do you still miss her?" she asked.

"Who, your mother?"

TJ nodded.

He smiled. "Every minute of every day. You?"

"Yeah," she said, her voice growing hoarse with emotion.

"That's why it's so important we spend time together as a family. Especially during this season." He hesitated, then added more softly, "We're all each other has."

TJ tried to answer, but her throat was too tight to speak. Instead, she gave a little smile and headed for the hallway again.

"Good night, kiddo," he said. She could feel him watching her as he quietly added, "I love you."

Her eyes burned and she could not face him. But she did manage to croak out a faint "I love you too, Daddy," before she disappeared around the corner.

And she did love him. More than he would ever know. At least until Christmas Eve, which was when they opened their presents. Because then he would know. In just a few short days, when he opened up the biggest wad of cash he'd ever gotten as a gift, he'd know for sure.

CHAPTER SEVEN

Another Day, Another Job

TIME TRAVEL LOG:
Malibu, California, December 21

Begin Transmission:
Tuna and I agree: Santa suits are not our subject's best look.

End Transmission

By the time TJ got to bed, she managed to squeeze in a whole 23½ seconds of sleep before her alarm went off for school. (It might have been 23¾ seconds, but how do you know how long you've slept if you've slept through it?)

Anyway, it was the last day of school before vacation, and things were a total blur.

First there was the minor problem of dressing herself. She didn't notice until she was in the school hallway that she'd put her socks on inside out. Luckily, no one paid attention. They were too busy snickering at her jeans, which were also inside out. But none of that bothered TJ. It's hard to be bothered by such details when you're busy sleepwalking.

Not only did she sleepwalk, she also managed to sleep-read her way through Ms. Grumpaton's English class and sleep-volleyball her way through Coach Steroidson's PE class (not as easy as you might think). Unfortunately, she wasn't so lucky when she sleep-flunked her way through Mr. Beaker's science test. It was on the eating habits of aardvarks. (What's up with Mr. Beaker and aardvarks, anyway?)

But none of that was as embarrassing as when Chad Steel (who was like a dream even when TJ wasn't sleeping) approached her locker.

"Hey, uh, um, er . . ." Even though they were next-door neighbors, Chad had a hard time remembering her name. Which was okay because when she was around him, TJ couldn't remember it either. He held up an iSlab he'd been typing on and asked, "Would you be interested in helping my church feed the homeless on Christmas Eve? We need to hire someone to deliver food from the restaurant. The pay won't be much, about $25."

"$25?" TJ croaked. From past experience, she knew it was risky to try to talk around Chad. (It's not that she couldn't talk; it's just that she always ended up blurting out such brilliant things as "You're gorgeous" or "I gotta go to the bathroom" or the ever-popular "I think I'm going to hurl!") But she figured she was only dreaming anyway, so what did it matter?

"Yeah," he said. "We were just going to pack sack meals and bring them over, but Hesper thought we should do more."

"Because it's Christmas?" TJ asked.

Chad glanced down, a little embarrassed. "No, because the newspeople will be there."

TJ should have guessed. Just like people needed air, Hesper needed cameras.

"Sure," TJ managed. She really wanted to shout, "Take me into your arms, you handsome hunk!" but figured, even for a dream, that might be pushing it.

"Great," he said. "I'll put you down for food delivery then." Once again he looked a little embarrassed. "I'm sorry—what is your name?"

"Oh, it doesn't matter," she said, drifting off into her semisleep mode.

He frowned. "I need to put something down."

"TJ would be nice," she mumbled.

He began to write. "TJ . . . and your last name?"

"Steel," she sighed dreamily.

He jerked his head up, surprised. "We have the same last name?"

She smiled. "Not yet."

"I'm sorry?" The tone of his voice startled her awake.

Realizing what she'd just said dreamily, she replied sternly, "No, no. *Your* last name is Steel. Mine is Finkelstein. TJ Finkelstein. Big difference. Please try not to make that mistake again."

"Right . . . sorry." He gave her an odd look and typed her name on the iSlab. "You'll be in charge of delivering the food."

"Great," TJ said. Then, desperately trying to remember the conversation she'd just slept through, she asked, "And what day was that, again?"

Chad cocked his head, even more puzzled. "Christmas Eve."

"Right, of course. Christmas Eve. And what type of food?"

He stopped typing.

She felt her face redden. "I'm sorry; I just have a lot on my mind. What did you say we were serving?"

He hesitated, then muttered something.

"I'm sorry," she repeated. "What did you say?"

He glanced up, his own face seeming to grow red. Finally he answered, "Cream puffs."

"Cream puffs?" TJ said in surprise. "For the homeless?"

Chad cleared his throat. "It was Hesper's idea."

"Cream puffs?" TJ repeated.

"Yeah," he muttered, then added, "stuffed with caviar."

"Caviar? Isn't that fish eggs?" TJ asked. "Something only the richest of the rich can afford?"

Chad nodded slowly.

TJ gave a shudder. "Inside the cream puffs?"

"That's right," he sighed. "We're serving them caviar cream puffs."

* * * * *

TJ hoped her next day at work would be better.

(She should have just hoped she'd survive it.)

For starters, Grumpy Claus never showed up. Rumor was that his parole officer said he was suffering from a bad case of allergies. TJ had her doubts.

If the man was allergic to anything, it was probably children. Either that or just being nice.

Fortunately for the department store, they'd found a substitute.

Unfortunately for TJ, it was TJ.

"You!" the assistant manager barked.

TJ turned from the hot chocolate machine in the employees' lounge as the woman shoved the Santa suit at her. "Try it on."

"Me?"

"Lazt night you zuccezfully handled zoze zcreaming ankle-biterz." (The assistant manager loved kids as much as Santa did.) "Zo zlip into ziz zuit."

"But—"

"And put on ziz beard."

"But—but—"

"Zee elaztic band goez up around your head."

"But-but-but—"

Ten minutes later (after TJ had quit her motorboat imitation), she was in the Santa suit and heading for the lobby to face the kids. "Okay, boys and girls, come and join me at—"

"OOOFF!"

"—Santa's throne and tell Santa what you'd like—"

"OOOFF!"

THUD

"—for Christmas."

The "Oooff!"'s were TJ stumbling and tripping.

The *THUD* was TJ falling face-first onto the floor, which was covered in fir boughs. And the reason she was falling face-first onto the fir-covered floor?

WARNING: DO NOT ATTEMPT READING ALOUD
IF YOU'VE RECENTLY RETURNED FROM THE DENTIST
(OR HAVE A MOUTH FULL OF CRACKERS)

TJ was falling face-first onto the fir-covered floor because falling face-first onto the fir-covered floor follows staggering with both legs in the same super-size suit leg.

(Too easy, you say? Okay, try this:)

And the situation that started her stumbling on the store's fir-covered floor with both legs in the same supersize suit leg is Santa's suit was twenty-two sizes too tall, making her size two too small by twenty sizes.

The good news is that's the end of the tongue twisters.

The better news is TJ finally made it to Santa's throne and sat down.

The bad news is with so much extra material for the suit, nobody could tell where her lap was.

"Mommy, Mommy," the first girl in line cried, "where do I sit?"

"Anywhere on that pile of red material," Mommy said. "He's gotta be in there somewhere."

And TJ was in there. Which explains why, for the next 4 hours and 32 minutes, she heard nothing but "I want this and I want that and I want more of this and I want way more of that."

Besides all that greed, there were also a few discipline problems.

"Hey, Santa," a little boy said (although it would have been easier to believe he was a boy if he didn't weigh 200 pounds and have a five o'clock shadow), "is this beard for real?"

"Ho-ho-ho," TJ groaned. (It's hard not to groan when you're being crushed by a 200-pound boy with a five o'clock shadow.) "Now don't go pulling Santa's beard," she warned.

"Wow, this elastic band holding it in place really stretches."

"I said, don't go pulling Santa's—"

SNAP

"YEOW!!!"

Then there was the matter of bathroom breaks. Not for TJ (she didn't get any), but for the cute little three-year-old who was so excited to see Santa that she took her break right there on TJ's lap.

"Ho-ho-ho!" TJ said, trying to be a good sport as she handed the soggy child back to her mother. "Looks like Santa's a Porta-Potty. Ho-ho-ho!"

And so the evening dragged on as little Jason and Julie and Heather and Harry kept making their Christmas demands. And even though TJ tried her best to pay attention, eventually all of the "I want this"-es and "I want that"-s started blurring into

"I want this and I want that and I want this and I want that and

I want more of this and I want
more of that and I want even more
of the more of this and I
want even more
of the more of that and
I want even more of the
more of the more of this
of the more more
of the more of I want even more
the more of the more of the more of

Finally nine o'clock rolled around and the store
closed. At last TJ was finished.

Well, not quite.

"Remember me?"

She looked down to see Number Too, still
wearing his Viking outfit. Beside him stood his sisters,
Number One and Number Thuree.

"Hi, guys," TJ said. She was so exhausted she
could barely stand. Still, she managed to be polite.
"Good to see you again."

They stood at her side saying nothing.

"Well," she said, turning toward the employees'
lounge, "I've got to get home. It's been a long day
and—"

"We fired her," Number Too said.

"Fired who?" TJ asked.

"Our nanny."

"Oh. Your mother fired your nanny?"

"No, *we* fired our nanny."

"You can do that?" As TJ spoke, she was surprised to feel Number Thuree reach up and quietly slip her hand into TJ's.

"We can and we did." The boy returned to playing his PSP.

TJ glanced around. "So . . . who's watching you now?"

"You are," he said without looking up.

"I'm sorry?"

"You are," he repeated. "If you want."

"Me?" she asked.

"Yeah, Number Thuree really likes you . . . and so do we."

TJ glanced at Number One, who nodded. "Well, thank you. I like you too, Too, but—"

"The money's really good."

"Money?" TJ asked.

"We'll pay you $100 an hour to watch us."

TJ gasped. "$100?!"

"All right, $150."

TJ would have liked to gasp again, but it's hard gasping when you've stopped breathing. It took several seconds before she was able to talk. "You would pay me $150 an hour to watch you?"

"Just until Momma gets home," he said.

"And when would that be?"

"Usually around midnight."

TJ glanced at her watch. That was three hours from now. And three hours times $150 came to . . . it was time for another gasp. Of course she was already overworked, and of course it would mean missing more family time with Dad, but the total came to $450!

"Are you sure about this?" she asked.

"Sure," Number Too said. "Just talk to our limo driver. He'll fill you in. And when Momma gets back, he'll take you home."

TJ's mind spun. Well, not really spun, more like repeated, *$450 . . . $450 . . . $450 . . .* Imagine her father's face when she gave him $450.

"So, what do you say?" Number Too asked.

What could she say? "Sure. Just let me get out of this costume and call my dad. $450, right?"

"Nah, that's too hard to remember," Number Too said as he continued playing his game. "Let's just round it up to an even $500."

CHAPTER EIGHT

TOO Much (In a WAY Too Much Kinda Way)

TIME TRAVEL LOG:

Malibu, California, December 21–supplemental

Begin Transmission:
Subject is so busy we barely see her. Luckily this gives us time to practice our comedy. I'm a zelph a minute. May give up my dreams of becoming a professional surfer and become a comedian!

End Transmission

TJ didn't want to say that Lady Goo-Goo's children were spoiled . . . but it was the nicest word she could find.

She thought there might be a minor problem when the back of their limo was filled with so many toys she couldn't see out the window. She knew there was a major problem when the limo pulled up to a mansion the size of Alaska. Actually, only the first floor was that big. The second floor was much smaller . . . about the size of Texas.

Things got even more interesting when they decided not to climb the 982 steps to the front door and took the escalator instead. The inside entry hall (which was only the size of New York—the state, not the city) had a giant fountain bubbling with soda pop.

"Is that . . . root beer?" TJ asked.

Number Too shrugged. "If it's Wednesday, yeah. We have a different flavor every day of the week."

Waiting for each of the children was their own electric car (complete with chauffeur) to take them down the long hallway to their playroom. TJ hitched a ride with Number Thuree, and once they arrived, she couldn't believe her eyes. The playroom was like a Toys 'R' Us store gone berserk. It's not that the kids had every toy you could imagine . . . it's that they had *three* of every toy you could imagine.

And yet, when she looked into the children's faces, she could see nothing but bored expressions and unhappiness. That is, when she could keep her eyes open long enough to see anything. It had been a long, long day.

"So," TJ said, fighting back a yawn and glancing at her watch. "It sure is getting late. What time do you guys go to bed?"

"Mwe won't mow woo mwed," Number One said as she took off her coat and dropped it on the floor. (Actually, it never quite made it to the floor, since a nearby butler dove and caught it before it hit the ground.)

TJ turned to Number Too. "What did she say?"

"'We don't go to bed,'" he said as he took off his Viking vest and another butler made a frantic catch. He continued toward a wall full of TV screens.

TJ followed him. "No bedtime?"

"Nah." He pointed at the remote on the table and a third butler scrambled to pick it up for him. "Momma loves us too much to make us go to bed."

TJ glanced at Number Thuree. The poor thing was so tired she could barely walk. This was obviously a new definition of love. But before TJ could say anything, Number One began screaming, "MWAUGH! MWAUGH! MWAUGH!"

They spun around to see the girl staring in horror at a tiny ball of dust in the corner. The first butler dashed over to help. But he was too late. By the time he had snatched up the dust ball, Number One was sobbing and shaking like a leaf.

Number Too snapped at the butlers. "Who's responsible?"

"The maid," the first butler answered.

"Tell her she's fired."

The butler bowed his head.

"And you are too," Number Too continued.

"But, sir, why?"

"Because I'm in a bad mood."

"Yes, sir."

"And you, too," he yelled at the second butler. "And you." He pointed at the third. "I'm in a *real* bad mood."

TJ shook her head in disbelief. And just when the weirdness couldn't get any weirder . . .

"Sweetie-kins!"

All eyes turned to the door as a mountain of gift-wrapped packages staggered inside. Somewhere underneath the mountain, TJ guessed there was another butler. And directly behind him stood Lady Goo-Goo. She wore a dress made of toothbrushes held together by (what else?) dental floss.

"MOMMA!" All three children ran to her.

"My babies!" Lady Goo-Goo said as she dropped

to her knees and gathered them into her arms. But before the children could even snuggle, she pulled away and rose to her feet. "It was so wonderful seeing you," she said, "but Momma's very tired."

"Oh, Momma," they started to whine.

"Tut-tut-tut." She held out a finger. "You know the rules, my sweets."

TJ watched as the kids seemed to wilt before her eyes.

"Yes, Momma," they mumbled.

"Momma's got to get her beauty rest," the woman said.

"Yes, Momma."

"But see, I bought you all these marvelous presents." She pointed to the moving mountain of gifts as it finally collapsed in the middle of the room.

"Yes, Momma," the kids said, barely bothering to look.

Once again, TJ felt a growing sadness. It was so obvious the gifts meant nothing to them.

"Well, good night, my babies," the woman said as she turned from the room. "Momma loves you oodles and oodles."

"We love you, too, Momma," they mumbled as she shut the door and disappeared from their sight.

TJ felt terrible as she observed this. Finally, to

break the mood, she walked over to the pile of gifts. "Well, it sure looks like you got a lot of stuff," she said, trying to sound cheerful. She picked one and added, "I wonder what this could be."

But none of the children answered. Instead, Number Too slowly drifted toward the wall of televisions. Number One walked back to the corner to make sure the dust ball was completely gone. And Number Thuree? She just kept standing there, staring at the closed door where her mother had been.

Feeling her own heart about to break, TJ cleared her throat and asked, "Well, what do you want to do now?"

"I think you better go home," Number Too muttered.

"Are you sure?" TJ asked.

"Yeah," he sighed. "Momma's here. Everything's good."

TJ looked back at Number Thuree, who was still staring at the door. "Really?" she said. "You call this good?"

"Yeah," he mumbled, "it's perfect." Without a glance at her, Number Too clicked on the televisions. "The chauffeur will pay you and take you home."

* * * * *

TJ didn't remember much of the limo ride home . . . just the part where she climbed in and laid her head back on the seat, and then the driver shaking her awake, saying, "Miss, you're home."

But she did remember the part about being $500 richer. Who wouldn't?

She also remembered dragging herself to the front door. This time there were no chain saws to greet her, no bikers, and no snoring fathers—just two goofballs from the 23rd century. And they weren't exactly waiting up for her. They were stretched out asleep, floating five feet above the top step on opposite sides of the stairway. Tuna wore one of those old-fashioned nightshirts with a long floppy hat, and Herby was in a pair of Winnie the Pooh pajamas with attached feet.

Since she wasn't in the mood for another lecture about being too focused on money, she tiptoed past the Christmas tree and up the stairs. She tried to squeeze between the guys and would have succeeded, if it weren't for the

crackle-snapple-popple

invisible force field she ran into. Suddenly every light in the house began flashing like a disco club. A mirrored ball even lowered from the ceiling and reflected colored lights in all directions.

Herby was the first to wake. "Hey, dude," he called to Tuna. "Look who finally decided to come home."

Tuna opened his eyes, spotted TJ, then stretched. "Oh, it's . . . it's . . ." He frowned. "What's her name again?"

Herby laughed. "That's a good one."

TJ was not amused. "Come on, guys," she whispered as she tried to

"ERRRR!"

and

"uUUuUGH!"

her way through the force field. "I'm really tired."

"Yeah, celebrating the holiday season can be rough," Tuna said.

"I'm not celebrating anything," TJ sighed.

"You can say that again."

"Another score!" Herby laughed and the boys high-fived. "You're one funny dude, dude."

Tuna shrugged. "I do my best."

"Come on," TJ whined. "Just let me go to bed."

"Hey, I've got one," Herby said. "You ready?"

"Let's hear it," Tuna said.

Herby gathered himself and took a breath. "Knock, knock."

"Who's there?"

"TJ."

"TJ who?"

"I can't remember. Can you?"

Tuna stared at him.

Herby grinned.

"You call that a joke?" Tuna asked.

"Guys," TJ begged.

"Admit it," Herby argued. "It's a real crack-up."

"Guys, I want to go to bed and I want to go NOW!"

"All right, all right," Herby said. "Don't get all gur-roid on us." He opened the Swiss Army Knife and

HOoooga ... HOoooga
popple-Snapple-crackle

the force field switched off.

Giving them a withering look, TJ climbed the final step, turned, and started down the hallway.

The boys barely noticed.

"You didn't think that was funny?" Herby asked Tuna.

"Hardly."

"Okay, okay, how 'bout this? How many TJs does it take to screw in a lightbulb?"

"I don't know," Tuna sighed. "How many TJs does it take to screw in a lightbulb?"

"TJ who?!" Herby clapped his hands and burst out laughing. "Get it? TJ *who*?"

He was still laughing when TJ passed Violet's bedroom. Her sister's light was on, so TJ slowed to peek inside.

It was worse than she feared. Remember Violet's thermometer chart, showing how much money she needed to raise to buy the TV? Well, it was not only colored to the top, but Violet had drawn a big puddle at the bottom showing how much was overflowing.

"Wonderful," TJ muttered as she pulled back from the doorway and headed for her own room. "Just wonderful."

She was so tired, she didn't bother to turn on

the lights or even change clothes. She just staggered to the bed and dropped onto the mattress. But the mattress was a lot lumpier than she remembered. Not only was it lumpy, but the lumps talked.

"OW!" they cried in a voice that sounded a lot like her littlest sister.

"Dorie?" TJ said. "Is that you?"

The lumps squirmed.

"What are you doing here?" TJ asked.

"I can't breathe," Dorie gasped.

"Oh, sorry." TJ rolled off her and to the other side of the bed.

Dorie took a deep breath. "I missed you."

"Yeah, I miss you too," TJ said. "But why are you here?"

"It's the only place you come when you're home." Dorie curled into a little ball, snuggling in nice and close.

TJ definitely got the message. And it was stronger than any flashing disco alarms or 23rd-century comedians. "Yeah," she said, "I've been kinda busy. But it'll all be over in a few days. And come Christmas Eve, I'll be giving Daddy the best gift he's ever had."

But Dorie didn't answer.

TJ gave her a nudge. "Squid? You awake?"

Her only answer was Dorie's slow, heavy breathing. She'd already drifted back to sleep.

TJ gave a weary sigh and moved in closer. It was nice to be next to someone who loved her so much . . . and whom she loved. Of course she could never tell Dorie that. After all, she was the big sister, and she had a reputation to keep up. But it felt good to snuggle next to her . . . no matter how freezing her little iceberg feet were.

CHAPTER NINE

Old Friends Drop In

TIME TRAVEL LOG:

Malibu, California, December 24

Begin Transmission:

Subject still not getting Christmas. We want to help, but some things have to be learned the hard way. In our subject's case, the VERY hard way.

End Transmission

One day dragged by after another until it was the afternoon of Christmas Eve—the last day TJ had to work. It was also the day for Chad and Hesper's "Feed the Homeless" program. But unfortunately

for the couple, things were not going well in a very
unwell sort of way. For starters, Chad had a long
talk with the minister of his church. For finishers,
Chad had to give Hesper (and her posse of Hesper
wannabes) the bad news.

"What do you mean he won't serve caviar cream
puffs?" Hesper demanded.

"Yes," her wannabes repeated, "what do you
mean?"

"He just thinks there's better food to feed them,"
Chad said.

"The caviar puffs cost $39.99 apiece. What could
be better than that?"

"Yeah," her posse repeated, "what could be better
than that?" (Instead of a posse, Chad wondered why
Hesper didn't just buy a bunch of parrots.)

He braced himself to give even more bad news.

"He also thinks we're somehow missing the spirit
behind the evening."

"The spirit?" she asked.

"You know, baby Jesus, peace on earth, goodwill
to men—that sort of thing."

"Oh, he's right!" Hesper nodded enthusiastically.
"Absolutely! Bernie already thought of that."

"He did?" Chad asked hopefully.

"You bet. That's why we're bringing in a giant snow machine."

Chad frowned. She still hadn't exactly grasped the reason for the season.

"And later, when the orchestra starts playing the Hallelujah Chorus, I'll fly down in all my glory. Then I'll walk amid those poor, wretched souls and feed them my caviar puffs." She clapped her hands. "Won't that just be fantasmo?"

"Yes!" Her wannabes clapped. "Fantasmo!"

Chad swallowed. "I'm not sure that's such a great idea."

"Oh, you're so sweet," Hesper said, linking her arm through his. "But don't you worry. I'll have plenty of bodyguards in case any of them want to touch me with their filthiness." She gave a shudder, which meant all her wannabes shuddered.

Hesper was definitely not making this easy. Still, Chad had to make sure she understood the church's concern. "Actually—" he cleared his throat—"the reverend thinks it's all just a little too much."

"Too much?" Hesper asked.

"He's afraid it'll make the people feel like we're just using them. Like they're somehow inferior to us."

"Well, of course they're inferior. Why else would they be homeless?"

"He doesn't see it that way. And to be honest, I don't either."

"Then maybe you two need to start seeing things differently," Hesper said. "Honestly, how else does he expect to get on prime-time television?"

Chad shrugged. "He doesn't. He just wants to remind the community that there are people less fortunate and we should pitch in to help them."

"Well, if he doesn't like the way I'm pitching in, maybe he can just do it himself."

"No, he still wants to work with you, but—"

"Maybe I don't want to work with him."

"Hesper—"

"Besides, we've already notified the press. All my fans will be watching. So if your church doesn't want to be part of the show, they can go somewhere else and put on their own."

Chad looked at the ground. He hadn't wanted it to come to this.

Seeing his expression, Hesper debated whether to yell and throw a fit or just break into uncontrollable sobs. Since she was a professional, she decided to do both. "If (*sob-sob*) they would rather do some pathetic little program instead of working with sweet, famous me (*stomp a foot here*), then they can just go ahead and (*sob-sob*) . . . they can just go ahead and (*stomp*

another foot) . . . they can . . . they can . . ." Hesper
could go no further. She had worked herself into
such a fury that she rolled her eyes up into her head
and collapsed into the arms of her wannabes . . .
who quickly rolled their own eyes and collapsed into
each other's arms.

Chad looked on. It was quite a performance. He
knew there would be no changing her mind, not
when she got like this. The program would go on
just as she had planned. And if his church wanted
to hold something less flashy, they'd have to find
someplace else to do it. There was no question
about it.

Unfortunately this led to an even bigger question.
Which program would Chad be part of? Sadly, he
already knew his answer. And sadder still, he knew
Hesper would be even less pleased.

* * * * *

TJ was dealing with a big question of her own.

Could she make it the entire day playing Santa
Claus while running on autopilot?

So far, she'd done okay. She'd managed to

"Ho-Ho-Ho!"

her way through the morning hours while half a trillion kids (give or take a billion) sat on her lap reciting their same worn-out

"I want this and I want that."

And she managed to

"MeRry ChRiStMaS!"

her way through the afternoon hours with another half-trillion critters of greed.

Of course there were the usual

SNAP

"YeOW!!!"-ings

and

"Listen, honey, next time could you use the bathroom before sitting on Santa's lap?"-ings

116

But as long as TJ kept her mind on all the money she was making, she did just fine. By the end of the day, she figured she would have:

Department store
(25 hours x $10 per hour) = $250.00

Babysitting Lady
Goo-Goo's children = $500.00

Delivering food to the
homeless tonight = $ 25.00

GRAND TOTAL: $775.00

That was a ton of cash. And already she could picture handing it over to Dad as they sat around the Christmas tree tonight. Talk about a moment to remember. Yes, sir, things couldn't have been better.

Actually, they could have been just a little better, if during the last 20 minutes the store was open, she hadn't seen Violet passing by with two hulking deliverymen. The men carried a huge cardboard carton with lettering on the side that read:

Eat Your Hearts Out
This TV Screen Is Way Bigger Than Yours

TJ went cold (and it had nothing to do with the rainbow snow cone little Josie had just spilled down her front). Instead, it had everything to do with Violet's buying a TV that obviously cost more than TJ's measly $775.00.

There was no question about it: TJ had to make more money and she had to make it fast!

But how?

Luckily (or unluckily, if you've read enough of these stories) the answer came sooner than she expected. Her cell phone began playing the love song from *High School Musical 17*. This, of course, was the ringtone she'd programmed for Chad Steel's calls.

Leaping to her feet, she dug the phone out of her pocket while dumping little Josie onto the floor. (Hey, we're talking Chad Steel here.)

"Hello?" she answered.

"Hi, uh, um, er . . ."

"TJ?" she said, helping him out.

"Yeah, TJ. Listen, I've got some good news and some bad."

The good news had obviously happened—she'd received a call from Chad Steel. She braced herself for the bad.

"I won't be helping Hesper with feeding the homeless tonight."

"Why not?" TJ managed to croak.

"My church wants to hold a smaller, quieter version at their place."

TJ's heart sank to her stomach. "So . . . you don't need my help?"

"I don't think so."

Forget the stomach. Now her heart was on the floor swimming in melted rainbow snow-cone juice.

"But Hesper still does."

"Oh," TJ said, as if that was supposed to make her feel better.

"And she might be willing to pay more."

Suddenly TJ *was* feeling better. "Really?"

"So if you're interested, you can still go to the restaurant and pick up the caviar puffs."

"Cool," TJ said.

"But you better hurry. It's almost time."

She glanced at her watch. "I've got just a few more minutes here at the store."

"Great. I'll let Hesper know. And, JT?"

She figured that was close enough. "Yeah?"

"Thanks. For Hesper, I mean. She needs all the help she can get."

You're telling me, TJ thought. But she managed to answer, "Sure, no problem."

"I'll see you later, then."

"Sure, no problem." TJ winced. *Sure, no problem?* What kind of answer was that? But before she could worry herself into an ulcer, she was startled by

"YOOOW . . .

WAAA-HAAA!"

as Number Too, still wearing his Viking costume, swung into the lobby on a rope and dropped down in front of all the waiting mothers and children.

Everyone was stunned into silence. Well, they were stunned into silence until he drew his sword and began swinging it and shouting, "Stand back or I vill eat you all vor me supper!"

That pretty much took care of the stunned silence. It's hard being stunned silent when you're busy screaming, "THE CRAZY VIKING BOY IS GOING TO KILL AND EAT US ALL!"

"What are you doing?!" TJ shouted at Number Too.

"I'm playing Viking!"

"This lobby is not your playroom!" she shouted back.

"It is now!"

"Since when?"

"Since we couldn't decide what we wanted for Christmas, so Momma bought us everything!"

"Your mother bought you everything in the store?"

"No. She bought us the store."

TJ's mouth dropped open. "Where is she? Where is your mother?!"

"She's not here."

"Why not?"

"We told her you'd look after us!"

CHAPTER TEN

Check, Please

TIME TRAVEL LOG:

Malibu, California, December 24—supplemental

Begin Transmission:
Subject learned the high cost of big business
(plus how to dog-paddle in a Santa suit).

End Transmission

Actually, Number Too got it wrong. Lady Goo-Goo hadn't bought the whole store. She'd just rented it . . . for the whole evening.

"So we'd have something to do," Number Too explained.

"But it's Christmas Eve," TJ said. "Aren't you going to spend it with your mother?"

"Nah, she's got too many parties to go to. But that's okay—there's plenty we can do here."

And they wasted little time.

First there was Number One's joy of finding the fire alarm and

BA-RAAAAAAAANG

pulling it.

Suddenly everybody was running back and forth and forth and back in major, big-time panic. Because more than just the alarm sounded. The overhead sprinklers also began

HISSSSSSSSsss-ing

as the world's biggest indoor rainstorm began.

"What iz happening?!" the assistant manager shouted as she sloshed into the lobby.

TJ spotted Number One and ran to her. "What did you do that for?" she shouted over the rain and the alarm.

"Mwere's mwoo mwany mwerms!" Number One yelled through her mask.

"There's what?" TJ shouted.

Number One pointed at the computer game display and yelled, "Mwoo mwany mwerms!"

The weird thing was TJ actually started to understand her. "Too many germs?"

Number One nodded and pointed to the computer game display again.

"So you're washing them?" TJ shouted. "You're washing the keyboards?!"

Number One nodded even bigger.

TJ was about to yell something kind and sensitive like *"Are you nuts?!"* but she was interrupted by an even louder

WhOOoosh

She spun around to see cute little Number Thuree (complete with her cute little snorkel and swim mask) standing by another wall. She had just opened the valve to one of several giant water pipes, causing a wave of water, slightly larger than the Atlantic Ocean, to flood across the floor. And Number Too, being the helpful big brother, came to her aid and started opening valves on the other pipes.

"WHAT ARE YOU DOING!?" TJ yelled as water quickly rose from her feet to her ankles, then to her knees. But as she watched Number Thuree push off into the water and begin snorkeling through the store, she already had her answer. If Number Thuree couldn't play in her bathtub at home, she'd make a bathtub out of the store!

Soon the water was up to TJ's waist. And just so Number Thuree wouldn't have all the fun, Number Too raced to the nearby sporting goods department and grabbed a canoe paddle. He spotted a sofa floating out of the furniture department, leaped onto it, and began shouting more cheery Viking phrases like "I HAF COME TO PILLAGE AND DESTROY YOUR COUNTRY!"

"Number Too!" TJ yelled.

But it did no good. He paddled toward customers, swinging his sword and shouting, "PILLAGE AND DESTROY! PILLAGE AND DESTROY!" as the customers swam for their lives, screaming, "WE'RE ALL GOING TO DIE! WE'RE ALL GOING TO DIE!"

They might have been more relaxed if Number Thuree hadn't kept swimming under the water behind them and grabbing their legs.

"SHARKS!" they screamed. "WE'RE ALL GOING TO DIE AND THEN BE EATEN BY SHARKS!"

"Don't be ridiculouz!" the assistant manager shouted. "It'z juzt a little water. You're perfectly zafe!"

"OH YEAH?" a mother shouted as she pointed to a woman's arm floating by. "TELL THAT TO *HER*!"

"OR HER!" another screamed, pointing to a bobbing head.

(Of course they were just department store dummies broken apart by a fake Viking with a fake sword. But there was no convincing the moms.)

So . . . for those of you keeping score (and who happen to be movie buffs), we have

1 *Perfect Storm* raining from the ceiling
1 *Jaws* nibbling at the backs of people's legs
1 *How to Train Your Dragon* Viking
More body parts than a creepy horror movie
More screaming people than a bad zombie movie
And a shouting assistant manager who still
    resembles King Kong

"WHO IZ REZPONZIBLE?" she began yelling. "WHO IZ REZPONZIBLE?!"

Since snorkeling sharks and rampaging Vikings are not good at answering questions, the assistant manager approached Number One, who was having the time of her life at the computer games. She had peeled off her mask and gloves and was playing one keyboard while the other keyboards around her were shorting out with more sparks than the Fourth of July.

"Where iz your mother?" the manager demanded.

Number One glanced up from the games and shook her head.

"Zhe'z not here?!" the manager asked.

Number One nodded.

"THEN WHO IZ REZPONZIBLE?"

Number One glanced at TJ and pointed.

TJ turned to the assistant manager and smiled.

The assistant manager turned to TJ and glared.

* * * * *

Nearly two hours passed before they were able to silence the alarm, shut down the valves, and drain the water. By then TJ's phone had rung 336 times. The first time had been the dreamy love song from *High School Musical 17*.

"I know, I know—I'm late," she told Chad as she wrung water from her giant Santa suit, "but we had an emergency."

"It's okay," Chad said. He had phoned from the church, where they were feeding a handful of people who had stopped by. "But Hesper's been calling me like every 20 seconds. Can I just tell her to call you?"

"Sure," TJ said.

Naturally, this made Chad's life a lot easier, while making TJ's life . . . Well, that would explain why her phone was currently ringing for the 337th time. (And in case you're wondering about the ringtone . . . it was the Wicked Witch's theme from *The Wizard of Oz*.)

Once again TJ picked up and once again she was greeted by Hesper's hysterics. "Where are you?! The caviar puffs are waiting to be picked up at the restaurant!"

"I told you, I'll be right there," TJ said. "Just as soon as I find the children."

Actually, finding Number Too was easy. She just followed the trail of dummy arms, legs, and decapitated heads.

Number One was also easy to find. Since the girl had lost her gloves and face mask, TJ just followed the smell of cleaning supplies to the janitorial closet and found Number One busy

HO-HO-NOOO!

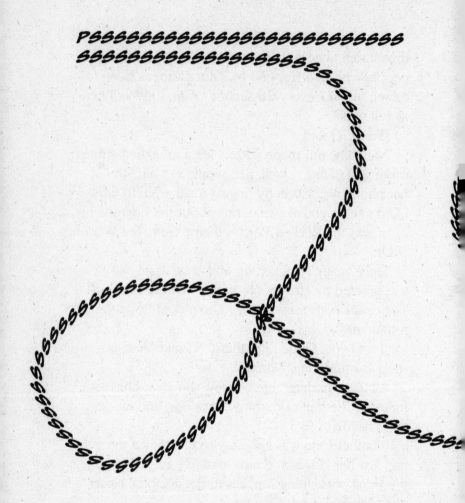

PSSSSSSSSSSSSSSSSSSSSSSSSSSSSS
SSSSSSSSSSSSSSSSSSSSSSSSS

ssssssss-ing

disinfectant in every direction.

Number Thuree was a little harder to find. But after checking every place that could hold water, they finally wound up in the ladies' restroom. The good news was Number Thuree was not in the toilet bowl. The not-quite-so-good news was she was sitting in the back tank. Granted, it was a little cramped, but some water to dive in was better than no water.

Finally there was the matter of TJ getting paid.

"PAID?!" the assistant manager roared as she motioned to the water damage around them. "You muzt be kidding."

"But it wasn't my fault," TJ argued.

"If you are in charge az zey zay, zen it iz mozt *definitely* your fault."

"But they're Lady Goo-Goo's children."

"Zat iz between you and her."

TJ didn't like this, not one bit. She'd worked too hard for that $250. "You're going to keep some of my money until I talk to her?" she demanded.

"I'm going to keep *all* your money until you talk to her. And I will be zending your parentz zee bill for the rezt."

If TJ's jaw dropped any lower, it would have bruised her toes. A giant repair bill was *not* the Christmas gift she wanted to give Dad.

She would have argued longer, but the Wicked Witch's theme began its 338th ring. She had to get going. Losing all that hard-earned money did not make her happy, but if her math was right, she still had $525, which was better than nothing.

She led the children outside—spraying the air all around Number One with disinfectant and tugging at Number Thuree (who kept gazing longingly at the larger mud puddles).

"Where's your chauffeur?" TJ asked Number Too.

"We sent him home," he said.

"You what?"

"I told you, we rented the store for the whole night."

TJ sighed. "All right, all right. Then I guess we'll take a bus."

The children stared at her.

"What?" TJ said.

"A . . . bus?" Number Too asked.

"Yeah, you know, a bus," TJ said.

All three continued staring at her.

"You do know what a bus is, right?"

More staring.

She tried again. "A big, long thing with lots of people inside?"

Number One's eyes widened in fear. "Germs!"

Number Too lowered his voice. "You're not actually talking *public transportation*, are you?"

"Well, yeah."

He shook his head. "We don't mingle with the public."

"Right," TJ answered, "unless it's to attack them as Vikings or sharks."

The kids looked at her in silence.

"All right, all right . . ." TJ threw up her hands. "A taxi. We'll take a taxi."

More looks.

"You do know what a taxi is?"

"We've seen them on TV," Number Too admitted.

"Good. I'll call a taxi. It'll take us to the restaurant, we'll drop off the food, and then I'll run you home." She glanced at Number One, who was still trembling. "And don't worry." She held up the disinfectant. "I'll spray the seats."

Ten minutes later they were in a cab pulling up to the fancy French restaurant, Costz-way Tu'much.

"That'll be $25," the cab driver said.

TJ was stunned. "You drove less than a mile."

"Welcome to Malibu, toots."

She dug into her pocket, pulled out the money, and handed it to the cab driver. Now she was down to $500.

"What, no tip?" the driver asked.

Make that $490.

"Will you wait here until I get the food?" TJ asked him.

"For another $20."

(That's $470 for you math geniuses.)

TJ and the kids climbed out of the cab and entered the back of the restaurant, where they were greeted by Chef Hugo Ego.

"It is about time," he growled. "My assistants have had the caviar puffs prepared for over an hour."

"Sorry," TJ said as she dragged Number Thuree past a giant and very inviting cauldron of French onion soup.

"I will not allow my masterpieces to be served if they are not at the peak of freshness."

"I understand," TJ said as they rounded the corner and she saw the entire wall stacked with small plastic boxes. "Are those them?"

"But of course."

"How many are there?"

"There are 1,350 works of art," he replied.

"I can't get them all into the taxi!" TJ exclaimed.

"I am an artist, not a delivery service."

TJ's mind raced, searching for a solution. "Wait! I've got it. Let's bring all the people over here."

"People?" Chef Ego frowned. "I thought they were the homeless."

"Right," TJ said. "People, homeless. They're the same thing."

Chef Ego's frown deepened a moment before he broke into laughter. "I see. You are making a joke. Yes, very funny. Very funny indeed." Before TJ could argue with him (or give him a good punch in the gut for being a jerk), he changed subjects. "Now, as far as transportation, you will note each delicacy is packed in its own container. This not only adds to the overall dining experience but protects their delicate shape during transport."

TJ's mind resumed racing. Transportation. She had to find a way to transport them. Finally, with no other solution in sight, she reached for her cell phone.

"What are you doing?" Number Too asked.

"I'm calling for more taxis. It's going to cost a bundle, but we need more taxis."

Chef Ego cleared his throat. "Speaking of cost . . . there will be an extra charge for the boxes."

TJ looked up from her phone in alarm. "Didn't Hesper Breakahart pay for them?"

"She paid for the caviar puffs, not the boxes—which

I might point out were specially designed for this occasion by a friend in Beverly Hills."

TJ swallowed hard. She knew she had to ask the question she didn't want to ask but had to ask because it was the question to be asked.

TRANSLATION: Uh-oh.

"How much will they cost?"

"Because it is for a good cause, and since it is Christmas, I shall give you a discount."

"Really?" TJ's face brightened.

"I shall charge you a mere $345 for the entire lot."

TJ's face clouded. If you math geniuses are still there, that left her with a grand total of . . . $125.

And the night was still young.

fling-fling-fling
SPLAT! SPLAT! SPLAT!

TIME TRAVEL LOG:

Malibu, California, December 24–supplemental
of supplemental

Begin Transmission:
*Have encountered slight glitch with force field.
Unable to assist subject at this time. With luck,
she will survive without our brilliant assistance.
Then again, we all know about her luck (and
our brilliance).*

End Transmission

TJ's fleet of taxis (all four of them) raced through
the streets. It was eight o'clock. She'd already missed

Christmas Eve dinner with her family. Now she had to unload the food and rush home before she missed everything. *"We'll be able to focus on more important things, like spending time with one another."* Wasn't that what Dad had said? If she didn't hurry, she couldn't even do that!

The taxis screeched to a stop in front of the tables that had been set up. TJ threw open her door, and just in time. Hesper Breakahart was being lowered on a cable from the helicopter—flapping her angel wings and waving her magic wand. (Apparently no one had bothered explaining the difference between angels and fairy godmothers.)

In any case, everything was there—the news cameras, the orchestra, and the snow machine, which was attached to a fire hydrant and pumping out its wet, snowy flakes all over the crowd.

Things couldn't be more perfect.

Except for the crowd. They hated it. Actually, they didn't hate the cameras, orchestra, or snow . . . they just hated Hesper. And the more she talked, the more they hated.

"You poor wretches!" she shouted from the air. "I have come to deliver you from your pathetic exis-tence!" She waved her wand toward TJ and the taxis.

"Behold, because of my great, giving nature, I have provided you my manna from heaven."

(Apparently no one bothered explaining humility to her, either.)

To make her point, the orchestra broke into a rousing rendition of the Hallelujah Chorus . . . as the crowd broke into a grumbling rendition of "Who does this chick think she is?"

But TJ barely noticed. She was racing around, unloading the taxis and setting out the caviar puffs. It would have been nice to have help, but Number One was too busy staring out the taxi window in terror, Number Too was too busy playing level 5,034 on his PlayStation, and Number Thuree? She'd found a nearby gutter where the melting snow was running off and she was splashing happily.

All this as Hesper continued her airborne greeting. "And so, thanks to my incredible generosity, I hereby **OOOFF!** I hereby **UGH!**"

The **OOOFF**s and **UGH**s came as the helicopter's cable kept sticking. It would lower her a foot and then jerk to a stop, then lower her another foot and stop. The more it jerked, the more she squirmed. And the more she squirmed, the more she began to swing back and forth.

But no one paid attention. They had all turned to the food TJ was setting out. Some had even started eating it . . . or trying to.

"Blah!" An older woman spat out her first bite. "What is this garbage?"

One of the news cameramen moved in for a close-up as another man gagged on his bite.

"They're caviar cream puffs," TJ explained.

"Caviar what?!" The woman sniffed at what was left in her hand . . . as the cameraman moved in closer and Hesper swung farther.

"I hereby *OUCH!*"

"Get that camera out of my face!" the old woman shouted.

"I hereby *AGHH!*"

"What does she think we are?" a man yelled as he threw his caviar puff to the ground. "This stuff isn't fit for animals."

"That's how she's treating us," another growled.

"Like animals," another agreed.

"We're her little pet project," another sneered.

"Get your camera out of my face!" the first woman repeated.

Things were definitely not going well in a very unwell kind of way. Not only were the people angry, but Hesper kept swinging closer and closer to the nozzle of the snow machine.

"You want a bite?" the woman yelled at the cameraman who still wouldn't leave her alone. "Then have a bite!" With that she

SPLAT!-ed

the caviar puff directly onto his lens.

Some of the crowd laughed . . . until the cameraman grabbed a puff off the table and

SPLAT!-ed

it into the woman's face.

Now everyone was laughing as another man grabbed a puff and shoved it into his neighbor's face. And then another one threw it into another face. And then another. Before you knew it, Chef Ego's delicacies were

fling-fling-fling-ing

through the air as a good, old-fashioned

SPLAT! SPLAT! SPLAT!

food fight began. (At least they discovered his food was good for something.)

Now everybody was *fling*-ing and *SPLAT!*-ing and having the time of their lives. Well, everybody but Hesper. The fairy godangel just kept swinging back and forth until she finally

CRASH!-ed

into the snow machine nozzle, completely snapping it off.

No problem . . . except for the water that began *gush*-ing from the broken nozzle. And we're not talking a little *gush*-ing. We're talking a major

GUSHHHHHHHH-ing

Within seconds the place had more water than . . . well, than a Bags Fifth Avenue department store on Christmas Eve.

But no one cared as the caviar puffs continued to

fling-fling-fling

and

SPLAT! SPLAT! SPLAT!

Yes, sir, it was a great time . . . until a little voice began screaming, "Help me! Help me!"

TJ spun around to see Number Thuree. The water had roared down the gutter and was washing her away. She was heading directly for a drain opening under the sidewalk . . . an opening big enough for her tiny body to slip through and be swept away forever!

Before TJ could react, Number One was out of the taxi. Forget the crowd; forget the germs—that was her little sister and she wasn't going to let anything happen to her.

But she was too slow.

Number Thuree screamed as the water swept her the last few feet and washed her down into the drain.

Washed her down . . . but not away.

At the last second, a skin-and-bones homeless kid

had appeared. With lightning speed, he had leaped into the drain and caught the little girl.

Caught her . . . but not saved her.

Because now, like Number Thuree, he was also inside the drain. He had managed to grab the edge and cling to it with one hand, while holding the girl with the other. But as the water beat down on top of them, his grip was slipping. Still, he would not let go of her. Even if it meant being washed into the storm sewer with her, he would not let go.

"Climb on top of me!" he shouted over the roaring water. "Climb onto my shoulders!"

But Number Thuree was too terrified to move as she kept screaming, "Help me! Help me!"

Finally Number One arrived. For the briefest moment, the big sister hesitated. The water was black with filth and sludge. There was no telling how many billion germs were in it. But she saw no other way. Trembling with fear and summoning all of her courage, Number One slowly knelt in the rushing water. It flooded and splashed all around her.

Stretching her arm down into the raging torrent, she yelled, "Grab my hand!"

Number Thuree looked up, her eyes wide in fear.

"Grab her hand!" the boy yelled. "Climb onto my shoulders and grab her hand!"

The water grew deeper and swifter by the second. Any moment the current would become too powerful for the kid to hang on. Any second, he and Number Thuree would be swept away, down and under the street.

"Do it!" Number One shouted as water flooded around her, splashing into her face, even into her mouth. "Hurry!"

Finally, very carefully so she would not slip, Number Thuree began climbing up the boy's chest.

"That's it!" Number One shouted. "Keep climbing!"

"You can do it!" the boy yelled over the roaring water. But even as he shouted, his grip was weakening.

"You're almost here!" Number One yelled.

As Number Thuree climbed, the boy adjusted his weight, trying to brace himself. But it was a losing battle. His fingers started to slip. And then, just before they gave way, Number One took a deep breath and stuck her face into the muddy torrent. It took forever, but at last she came up gasping and choking. And in her arms was her baby sister.

Everyone broke into cheers and clapped as they moved in to help. Everyone but the boy.

He was nowhere to be found.

"Where is he?" the old woman shouted as she approached the drain.

More people arrived. Some knelt. Others dropped onto their hands and knees, peering into the opening. But gradually, one by one, they raised their heads and slowly shook them.

The boy was gone.

A heavy silence fell over the crowd. Everyone became very, very quiet . . . except for Hesper Breakahart. She was too busy fixing her hair and checking for broken nails to have noticed what happened.

"Come on, everybody," she called as she approached the tables. "Dig in."

TJ couldn't believe her ears.

Neither could anyone else as they slowly turned and stared at the TV star.

But Hesper was completely oblivious. "They're really, really yummy," she said as she cranked up her smile to ultrafake.

No one smiled back.

Then, from somewhere in the back of the group, TJ heard a shout.

"There he is! There's the boy!"

The crowd craned their necks. And there, climbing out of a drain a block away, was the skin-and-bones kid. He'd been washed underground for the entire block but somehow managed to grab the edge of the next drain and pull himself up.

Once again, cheers rose from the group and several raced down the street to greet him. He was jostled a bit as they raised him onto their shoulders, his hair dripping, his body covered in mud and goop.

Unfortunately, Hesper Breakahart was still too focused on . . . well, on Hesper Breakahart. "No need to thank me," she shouted over the cheers. "These yummy caviar puffs were the least I could do . . . and the most expensive. So just enjoy them and—"

fling

SPLAT!

"Mmwickk!" Hesper screamed as she reached up to wipe the gooey mess from her face . . . and to spit out a mouthful of fish eggs. "Look what you've done to my (*spit-spit*) makeup and to my expensively styled—"

fling-fling-fling

SPLAT! SPLAT! SPLAT!

"MMWICKK!" she screamed louder as she rewiped and respit. But the food fight had resumed. And this time there was no stopping it. Because this time, everyone had found a common

fling-fling-fling-

fling-fling-fling

SPLAT! SPLAT! SPLAT! SPLAT! SPLAT! SPLAT!

enemy. Within seconds Hesper looked like the Pillsbury Doughboy, covered from head to foot in gooey dough . . . with the beauty bonus of a billion smelly fish eggs.

TJ tried not to laugh (though not very hard) as she hustled the three children toward the taxi. She had to hurry and get home.

As they were climbing inside, her cell phone rang her favorite love theme. She pulled the phone from her pocket and answered, "Hello?"

"How's it going?" Chad asked.

"Not bad," she said, ducking a few

fling-fling-fling

stray caviar puffs.

"Great," Chad said. "Listen, we've got way more food here at the church than we know what to do with. Any chance of sending some of your people our way?"

TJ looked over the crowd. "Sure, I think we can send a few—

SPLAT!

mweople."

(Sometimes love slows down your ducking reflexes.)

"Terrific," Chad said. "Thanks!"

After hanging up and wiping her face, TJ turned to the group and gave them the news. From the clapping and excitement, she guessed they were in the mood for some real food. And despite Hesper's protests, they started for the church. As they left, TJ began to join the kids in the taxi. There was no time to waste. She had to get home. She had to give Dad the $125. It wasn't much, but $125 was better than—

"Hey, you! Girlie!"

All four of the taxi drivers she'd hired were standing in a line beside the cab.

"Where's our money?" the first demanded.

"Oh," TJ sighed. "Right. Sorry." She dug into her pocket. "How much do I owe you?"

"Let's see; the four of us at 25 bucks apiece—that comes to $100."

TJ's heart sank. Amazing. Unbelievable. After working herself to death all week, all she had left was a measly $25.

"And 20 bucks for tips."

Make that a measly $5. Not even enough for a taxi ride home.

* * * * *

By the time TJ and the three children had trudged to her house on foot, nearly another hour had passed. But for some strange reason, nobody was home.

Well, nobody from *her* century.

She'd barely stepped through the front door before she saw the boys. They sat working in front of a giant pile of broken electronics at the foot of the stairs. Broken electronics that were mixed in with what was left of one very destroyed Christmas tree.

"Tuna? Herby?" she cried. "What happened?"

Tuna looked up. He was covered with tape from head to toe. Come to think of it, so was Herby. Glancing across the pile of electronic gizmos and tree branches, he said, "Apparently, one of us forgot to disengage the force field at the top of the stairs."

"It wasn't me, dude," Herby said as he tried taping one of the broken pieces to another.

"Well, it certainly wasn't me," Tuna said as he tried jamming his own two pieces together.

"Well, it wasn't me."

"Well, it wasn't—"

"So what happened?" TJ interrupted.

Herby answered, "The delivery dudes were kinda carrying your dad's TV up to his room when they kinda ran into the force field and dropped it, and it kinda bounced down the steps and crashed into your Christmas tree and kinda turned into . . ." He motioned to the pile of broken branches and electronics.

"That's the TV set Violet bought?" TJ asked in astonishment.

"*Was*," Tuna corrected.

Herby let out a whoop as he successfully taped

his pieces together . . . well, successfully except for also having his fingers taped to them.

Meanwhile, Number Too and his sisters had crowded into the room. "Hey!" the boy demanded. "Where are those voices—?"

Without bothering to look, Herby struggled to reach into his pocket, pulled out the Swiss Army Knife, and

zzoo . . . o . . . o . . . . a . . . . . a . . . . . a . . . . h . . . . h . . . .

froze the children in time.

(Well, not really *froze*, more like slowed them down in an it-will-take-forever-for-the-kid-to-finish-his-sentence kind of way).

"—cooomiiiiiiiiiinggggg froOooooooooommmmmmmmm?"

"No need to worry," Tuna said, as he returned to jamming his two pieces together . . . until they exploded into a dozen more, smaller pieces. "We will have this repaired in no time." Giving up, he tossed the pieces over his shoulder to a growing discard pile and reached for a couple more.

"That's right, no prob," Herby said as he success-fully removed his fingers from his taped pieces . . . only to discover he'd now taped his foot to them.

"So where did everybody go?" TJ asked. "Where are Dad and Violet and Dorie?"

"Violet was majorly bummed about the TV," Herby said.

Tuna added, "And Dorie was rather distraught about the destruction of the Christmas tree."

"So?"

"So with neither a tree nor presents, your father thought he'd cheer them up by taking them to church. Apparently they were holding some sort of dinner there. You'll find a note on the table."

TJ dragged her exhausted body across the room to the table. "This is the worst Christmas ever," she grumbled. "It'll probably take another hour to get there and I'm so tired I can barely—"

Before she finished her sentence, she heard a clear and distinct

Chugga-chugga-chugga

BLING

which, as everyone knows, is the sound made when you are transported across town by a 23rd-century Transporter Beam shooting from a 23rd-century Swiss Army Knife.

CHAPTER TWELVE

Wrapping Up

TIME TRAVEL LOG:

Malibu, California, December 24—supplemental of
supplemental of . . .

Begin Transmission:

*Thanks to our brilliant brilliance, ingenious genius,
and humbling humility, our subject has learned her
lesson. This time.*

End Transmission

"TJ!"

She spun around to see little Dorie running at her
full speed.

"No, Squid, don't. I'm too tired to catch—

SLAM

you."

As Dorie landed in her arms, the two

Stagger, Stagger, stagger-ed

backward until they landed in someone else's arms.

"Whoa, you okay?"

TJ turned to see that she was being held by (insert dreamy sigh here) Chad Steel. He wore an apron and stood behind a long table, where he was serving mashed potatoes and gravy.

"Yikes," she sorta screamed as she scrambled out of his arms. She would have stayed there forever, but there was something about a church full of people staring at her that made it feel a bit awkward. Then there was the minor detail of her father standing directly beside them.

"Daddy?!" This time she really did scream.

"Hi, sweetheart." He grinned. He was wearing his own apron and holding a serving spoon. "I didn't see you come in."

"Oh," she squeaked as her eyes shot back and forth between Dad and Chad like she was watching a tennis match. "I just sort of, you know, *popped* in."

Dad nodded and motioned to Chad. "I see you've met our next-door neighbor."

"Hey." Chad smiled.

TJ felt her face growing hot.

Chad motioned to the crowd of people. Some were still in line. Others sat or stood in small groups, eating, talking, and seeming to have a great time. Most were the street people who had come over from Hesper's Christmas catastrophe, though there were plenty of church folks, too. "Thanks for sending them our way," Chad said.

TJ peered out over the crowd and nodded.

"Did you see our Christmas tree?" little Dorie asked. She pointed across the room, where a handful of people were decorating a tree and chattering away.

"TJ," Dad asked, "are you okay? You look really tired."

"It's been a long day," TJ sighed.

"So I heard."

"From who?"

"Chad here, for one. He says you've really been putting in the hours."

She threw a look at Chad, feeling her face burn all the hotter.

"Actually, he's been saying a lot of good things about you." With a twinkle, he added, "He's quite the fan. Isn't that right, Chad?"

Chad smiled good-naturedly.

If TJ's face was burning before, it was time to call the fire department now. She eyed her father, who was grinning warmly. Then she blurted out, "Oh, Daddy, I'm so sorry."

His grin faded and he looked puzzled. "For what?"

She felt her throat tighten. "I wanted so much for you to have a great Christmas. I mean, with Mom gone and all, I just wanted . . ." And then, before she could stop them, the tears came. Tears of exhaustion, of frustration, of disappointment. "I worked so hard so I could give you some money, you know, to help with the bills and everything." She dug into her pocket and pulled out the ragged $5 bill. "And now all I've got is . . . all I can give you is . . ." The tears came faster, and she couldn't continue.

"Oh, sweetheart . . ."

She gave her eyes a swipe, but it did no good. She knew Chad was watching, but she couldn't stop. "And Vi . . ." She gulped a breath. "I saw what happened to the TV she bought you. I wanted to give you a better present than hers, but now . . . now you've got . . . you've got . . ." The tears turned into sobs. Talk about embarrassing.

"Oh, TJ."

Try as she might, it was impossible to catch her breath. The week had been too long, the defeats too overwhelming. Before she knew it, her father was wrapping those big arms around her.

"I'm sorry," she choked. "Everything went all wrong."

"What are you talking about? Nothing went wrong."

"You were supposed to have the greatest Christmas ever. And now . . . and . . ."

"TJ . . . look at me."

She raised her eyes and saw his face wavering through her tears.

"I *am* having a great Christmas."

"But—"

"Look around you."

She glanced about the room—at the groups of people eating, talking, laughing. Even Violet seemed to be enjoying herself, chattering with a bunch of geeks who were no doubt creating a plan for world peace.

"*This* is what Christmas is about."

"But . . . you didn't get any gifts."

He motioned to the crowd. "What do you call this? Look at their faces, TJ. Look at the joy we get to be a part of."

Once again she scanned the room. It was true: everyone was having a good time—the homeless, the church members. Even Number One and the skin-and-bones kid who saved her sister. They were talking. Actually, more than talking—they were holding hands! (Though Number One was careful to keep a napkin between them.)

And Dorie? She'd found a new friend in Number Thuree. Not that Number Thuree talked that much, but it didn't stop Dorie. The little thing could do enough talking for both of them. Actually, she could do enough talking for the entire room.

"*This* is Christmas, sweetheart," Dad said. As he spoke, someone near the tree started to sing a carol.

"Hark! the herald angels sing,

'Glory to the newborn King.'"

Dad continued. "I know you miss Mom. I miss her too. But we have to go on." He gave TJ a little hug. "And isn't this how Christmas should be celebrated?

Being with the ones you love . . . and loving your
friends and neighbors as God loves them?"

The song grew louder as more people joined in.

"'Peace on earth, and mercy mild,

God and sinners reconciled!'"

TJ gave her eyes another swipe and glanced down.
Finally she began to nod. He was right. It had taken her
a while to see it and she'd definitely learned the hard
way, but he was right. Spotting the money in her hand,
she raised it halfheartedly. "And what about this?"

Dad smiled. He glanced around the room until he
spotted a small box at the end of the table. Someone
was dropping something inside it. When he stepped
back, TJ saw the word *Donations*.

She frowned, then looked at Dad. He gave her a
wink, his smile growing bigger.

And she had her answer.

Without a word, TJ slipped from his arms, walked
to the box, and dropped in the last of her hard-earned
money. As she did, the song grew even louder.

"Joyful, all ye nations, rise,

Join the triumph of the skies."

She returned to her father, who had started to sing along. Snuggling into the warmth of his arms, she also joined in.

"With angelic hosts proclaim,

'Christ is born in Bethlehem!'"

Across the room, invisible to everyone but TJ and still covered in cellophane tape, she spotted Tuna and Herby. They floated near the tree and were singing at the top of their lungs . . . completely off-key.

"Hark! the herald angels sing,"

They spotted her and grinned.

She grinned back, trying not to wince at their voices.

The boys gave her a thumbs-up and mouthed the words *Merry Christmas.*

She nodded, smiled, and returned the greeting. *Merry Christmas.*

Because it *was* a merry Christmas. Here, as she shared the love of her family, of her friends, and of people she didn't even know. Here, as everyone shared in God's love. Despite the problems, the mix-ups, and the mess-ups, it was quickly becoming one of TJ Finkelstein's merriest Christmases ever.

"'Glory to the newborn King!'"

Read all six wacky adventures in the

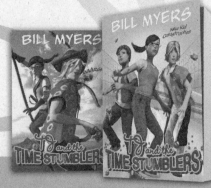 TJ *and the* TIME STUMBLERS series

#1 New Kid Catastrophes—*Available Now*

#2 Aaaargh!!!—*Available Now*

#3 Oops!—*Available Now*

#4 Ho-Ho-Nooo!—*Available Now*

#5 *Available Spring 2012*

#6 *Available Spring 2012*

RED ROCK MYSTERIES

BRYCE AND ASHLEY TIMBERLINE are normal 13-year-old twins, except for one thing—they discover action-packed mystery wherever they go. Wanting to get to the bottom of any mystery, these twins find themselves on a nonstop search for truth.

CP0140

Would you like Bill Myers

(author of TJ and the Time Stumblers series)

to visit your school?

Send him an e-mail:

Bill@billmyers.com